CAN ANYONE STOP THE INSECT INVADERS?

No, they're not the Mutant Spiders from Mars. Insect Invaders is the most popular computer game in America, but certain versions contain a deadly virus that fries hard drives like bacon and eggs!

Who created the virus and why? It's up to you and the Digital Detectives to find out.

To solve the case, you'll make on-line investigations of a creepy moonlit dock, a high-tech career fair, and a mysterious warehouse. Analyze every fingerprint, interrogate every suspect, and record everything in your on-line crime journal. Remember: if you miss a single clue, you might not live to solve another case!

DIGITAL DETECTIVES™
MYSTERIES

THE CASE
OF THE
KILLER BUGS

by Jay Montavon

RUNNING PRESS
Philadelphia • London

Copyright © 2000 by enhanceNOW.com

9   8   7   6   5   4   3   2   1
Digit on the right indicates the number of this printing

Library of Congress Cataloging-in-Publication Number 00-133409

ISBN 0-7624-0905-3

Digital Detectives™ developed by enhanceNOW.com, Carla Jablonski, and Jay Leibold

Designed by Bill Jones
Cover illustrations © 2000 by Mike Harper
Series Editor: Carla Jablonski
Running Press Editors: Jason Rekulak and Susan Hom
enhanceNOW Editor: Jason Zietz
Typography: Minion, Futura Condensed, Orbital

This book may be ordered by mail from the publisher. Please include $2.50 for postage and handling.
But try your bookstore first!

Running Press Book Publishers
125 South Twenty-second Street
Philadelphia, Pennsylvania 19103-4399

Visit us on the web!
www.runningpress.com

CHAPTERS

WELCOME DIGITAL DETECTIVE!

The first time you log on to the Digital Detectives web site,

http://www.ddmysteries.com

you will be required to choose a user name. Once you have received your user name, write it in the space below.

_____

Digital Detective User Name:

Your user name will bookmark your investigative work on the web site, so that you can continue where you left off.

WARNING:

This is *not* a typical mystery. You *should not* read every page of this book—that would spoil many of the story's best surprises! You will be directed on-line at certain points to gather evidence from the crime scenes. The web site will tell you which page of this book to return to. Do a good job and you'll solve the crime! Make a sloppy investigation and...well, some *very* bad things can happen...

Good luck!

1
JASON THE DESTROYER

Jason the Destroyer has a bead on a grasshopper, and it's a big one. You hold your breath. Exactly what does Jason have in mind for this bug?

The grasshopper jumps nervously from one end of the yard to the other, but Jason tracks it, his shoulders hunched. He licks his lips and peers through thick glasses at the twitching bug.

"Be careful," your friend Tina Garrett warns Jason. "If you eat the Queen, the whole horde comes after you." She huddles beside him, twirling a strand of her sandy-red hair into a knot.

"That's exactly what I want," Jason murmurs.

Jack Hertz catches your eye. "Grasshoppers don't have queens," he scoffs.

Jason pounces. Suddenly the grasshopper is huge, all eyes and spiny legs. It lets out a horrible shriek. The piercing sound is replaced by a hideous crunching as Jason stuffs the grasshopper into his mouth.

Jason lets out a satisfied sigh. He laces his fingers together, cracks his knuckles, and waits.

Now what? you wonder.

Then you hear a far off buzz. It grows closer and closer. Louder and louder.

"They're cooommmminng," Tina whispers.

A grasshopper jumps into the yard, then another and another. Jason pounces and gobbles them down. You watch his jaw open and clamp shut with each grab. More grasshoppers appear and Jason chomps down on them. Two, three, four at a time!

How can he keep at it? you wonder. The grass is dark with hoppers. Your stomach clenches as Jason keeps shovelling them in. He's gorging himself. The crunching roars in your ears. You're grossed out and awed at the same time.

Then all grows quiet again. The yard is free of insects.

Jason's score comes up on the computer screen.

INSECT INVADERS
Eat Or Be Eaten!
Player: Jason the Destroyer
Current rank: 1

Tina sits back. "Awesome," she breathes.

"Grotesque," Jack declares. Unlike Jason, Jack is not much into games. He thinks they're too easy.

Jason grins. "I don't know what that means, but I'm the champion of it."

Jason opens his web browser and logs onto the Internet to record his new feat with his fellow gamers. You watch as the logo of the company that makes INSECT INVADERS comes up on the screen.

Terrorstruck Games
A division of Cye-Tek

"Check it out," Jason brags. "I'm 253 points ahead of my nearest competitor."

"Yeah, but check *this* out," Jack counters. He grabs the mouse and clicks on a link at the bottom of the screen.

Uh oh. A message comes up warning that a new computer virus has been reported, and it might be related to the game.

"Players should download game extras *only* from the official INSECT INVADERS site," you read aloud.

"No bug's gonna get me," Jason asserts. He grabs the mouse back from Jack and surfs over to a site run by fans of the game. "I want to make sure everyone knows I'm still 'King of the Insectivores.'"

"Insectivores?" you repeat. You glance over at Jack. You know he'll know what the word means. He's better than a dictionary.

"Someone who eats insects," Jack explains.

As you watch Jason post a message about his latest exploits, you have to admit you feel a twinge of envy. INSECT INVADERS is a monster hit and Jason still hasn't let you play.

Okay, so he's really Tina's friend and you've only been over to his house twice. And you're still not even sure if a game where you eat bugs is exactly your idea of fun. But Jason could at least let you try it out. It's so expensive that you don't want to buy it unless you're positive you'll like it.

Jack peers over Jason's shoulder, reading the e-mail messages. "Looks like you've been challenged," Jack teases Jason. You check out the screen and read the new message.

To: KING OF NOTHING
You might think you're the King of the Insectivores but I'll bet you haven't even found the secret level.

"Secret level?" Jason says, worried.

Tina shrugs. "I haven't heard about any secret level."

As you watch Jason read more messages, you remember that you haven't checked your e-mail today. You ask Jason if you can pick up messages on his computer.

"Sure, just a sec." Jason clicks a few more times, then turns the computer over to you. He flops onto his bed, muttering about the supposed secret level.

You sit down and open the site where you get your mail. You find a new message. You don't recognize the sender's address.

To: freeboard
From: Skeet99
Subject:

11 tomorow night and be there on time. Dock 18. Dont bring no one else.

That's really weird. What is this message about? It doesn't make any sense. "Hey," you say. "Does anyone know this

Skeet99?"

Tina leans over your shoulder to read the message. "No, but he needs to go to English class more often."

Jack shakes his head, too. He nudges you out of the chair. "I'll do some research."

Jack takes over the computer like a race car driver sliding into a bucket seat. His fingers fly from the mouse to the keyboard and back. Web pages flash by, one after another, then pages of code, which he attacks with a flurry of typing.

Jack is, like, a genius. You know he'd ace INSECT INVADERS. He could probably *write* the game in about a nanosecond, if he wanted to. But he doesn't. He thinks games are kids stuff. Which is pretty funny, since he's thirteen, just like you.

Well, not exactly like you. Jack would rather spend his time inventing stuff. He comes up with amazing devices. His favorite at the moment is the headset that earned him his nickname, Satellite Jack. He can use it to receive e-mail, phone calls, and web pages. Even wearing the goofy thing, with his pudgy stomach, tight brown curls, and round, black-rim glasses on his round face, not too many kids dare to make fun of how geeky he looks. He's *that* smart.

"Hmmm," Jack grunts, stumped. "My guess is that he's not too computer literate. He doesn't have a clickstream to track across the Web. All I can tell you is that he lives here, in Crescent Bay. Probably some newbie who doesn't know the Internet from fishing gear."

"Whatever," Jason says, tugging at the chair. He's impatient to be back in charge.

Jack lets out a big, loud yawn and stretches his arms so that you all have to lean out of his way. "That's enough fun and games for me," he says. "Shall we move onto something more—*challenging?*"

Tina looks at her watch. "Nah, I've got to go home and make dinner for my dad." Tina lost her mom a few years ago, and her dad is a paramedic with odd hours. Tina is the only kid still at home, so she often has extra chores.

If she's going, you figure you'll go too. You don't know Jason all that well, and it's no fun just sitting watching him play INSECT INVADERS. Jack's not interested in hanging around anymore either.

The three of you thank Jason and gather up your stuff to leave. "Yeah, later," Jason mumbles, his face plastered to the screen.

Jack lives just over the ridge from Jason in the hills above town, in a big house with a view of the ocean. You and Tina live down in the flats, closer to the center of town.

"See you tomorrow," Jack says. He turns to head up the ridge. You all freeze when a scream of horror comes from Jason's second-floor room. You stare up at his window.

Tina laughs. "Jason probably just got eaten by a big fat caterpillar."

"I guess he's bugging now," you joke.

Jack rolls his eyes, then takes off. You grab your bike. Tina gets on her skateboard, and you head down the hill. The sun is just starting to set over the Pacific Ocean and the sky is a curtain of pink.

Tina's great. She's become one of your best friends since you moved to Crescent Bay in the summer. You hit it off right away because you're both board riders. She's a surfer and skateboarder, and back in Colorado you were pretty hot on the snowboard. Tina's been teaching you to surf, which she says is more exciting than snowboarding because it's like both you *and* the mountain are moving at the same time. She's something to see on her skateboard, with her chipped front tooth, green eyes, and wild sandstone-red hair flying out from under her baseball cap. She introduced you around to the other kids, making the move to California a little easier to take.

Crescent Bay was once a sleepy little city, known for its fishing industry and for the unusual crops farmers grew in the coastal valleys: artichokes, broccoli, and brussels sprouts. Lately, though, the town has been waking up, as high tech companies have begun moving in from Silicon Valley to the north. As a newcomer yourself, you can tell the locals aren't so thrilled about this. It brings more money and more jobs to the area, but it also disrupts the nice quiet pace of life.

"That e-mail message I got is kind of weird," you say to Tina as you head home. "Do you think it's for real?"

"Nah," Tina assures you. "I'll bet it's just a wrong number. I wouldn't worry about it."

But you do worry. Locals give you looks, like you don't belong here. Somehow they can tell that your parents work in high tech. It's like you're some kind of invader. What if one of them has it out for you?

"Maybe I should call Randy about it," you say.

Randy Rivers lives on your block. He's fourteen, and more the kind of guy you thought you'd meet in California: tall, muscled, athletic, with dark brown hair and bronze skin. Jack helps him run a web site called WhatISay.net. It's like an unofficial newspaper for your school and neighborhood.

"If you want," Tina replies. By now you've reached her street. She kicks up her skateboard. "Well, Dad's probably waiting. Later."

Dinner's ready when you get home. You decide not to bother Randy. You don't mention the mysterious e-mail to your parents, either. You eat, do some homework, and watch TV with your younger sister, Eve. After you brush your teeth, you go back online one more time.

Phew. No new messages.

You delete the strange e-mail so you won't have to look at it again in the morning. Then you go to bed, firmly decided you're not going to worry about Skeet99.

And you're right, you don't hear anything more from him.

For exactly 36 hours.

2
THE INVITATION

It stares you in the face two mornings later when you check your e-mail before school.

To: freeboard
From: Skeet99
Subject: last chance

Creep. I waited for you. But your lucky cuz Annie got delayed. She's coming in tonight. You better show up or dont show your face in town ever again.

Your hands shake a little as you forward the message to Tina, Jack, and Randy. You read it again. Why is this Skeet picking on you?

You shake your head. No. It can't be for me, you think. But you've got to find out. Sweat breaks out on your palms as you hit the reply key. With trembling fingers you type:

You must have the wrong person. I don't know anyone named Skeet. You must have sent this to me by mistake.

You don't sign your name, just in case. After you hit Send,

you let out a long breath. That ought to take care of it.

You get your books packed for school. You don't want to miss Randy. Usually you walk to school with him. You start for the door, then realize you forgot to log off.

When you go back to the computer, you've got new mail. Good, you think, Jack or Tina got your message.

"Oh no," you gasp. Your blood freezes when you see the sender's name. Skeet99 has already replied:

No, its for YOU.

"Oh man," you murmur. "Now what do I do?"

That clinches it. You're going to talk to Randy. He's older than you. He might have some idea of what to do.

You log off and dash out the door. Randy is already halfway down the street, so you run to catch up with him.

Before he can even ask you what's up, you spill out the story of the creepy e-mail.

Randy arches his brows. "Pretty whacked out," he agrees. "You scared?"

Your eyes drop to your sneakers. "A little bit," you admit.

"I don't blame you."

You glance back up. His deep brown eyes gaze back sympathetically. You were nervous that he'd think you were being a wimp. But all you see on his face is concern. You're glad you told him. You feel better already.

Tina rumbles up on her skateboard. She gives you each a swat on the head before making a U-turn in front of you and flipping the board up under her arm. You tell her about the latest e-mails.

"Ooh, Skeet's got attitude, doesn't he?" Tina remarks. "I wonder who Annie is. We should find out what's going on down at the docks.

Randy snaps his fingers. "Yeah, might be in-ter-esting."

Uh oh. You've seen that look before. Randy is always on the prowl for a good story to write up on his web site.

"Quit kidding around!" you say. "I don't want to be your latest news story." You turn to Tina. "Or *your* latest adventure."

They totally ignore your objections.

"We should check this out," Tina insists.

You frown at her. Sometimes you think all she lives for is the thrill she gets from dangerous situations. "It's not *your* life that's being threatened," you complain.

"Look, it's probably just a wrong address," Tina assures you.

"But what if it isn't? What if it's someone who doesn't like newcomers or high tech, and they want to make *me* their example?"

Randy waves a hand dismissively. "What was Crescent Bay before tech started coming in? 'Brussels sprouts capital of California.' Whoopee!"

"And broccoli, don't forget our broccoli," Tina puts in.

"Meanwhile, we've stumbled onto a good story," Randy says.

"Shouldn't I call the police?" you wonder.

Randy puts a hand on your shoulder. "They can't do anything yet. There's no evidence and Skeet hasn't harmed you in any way. Let's just go down to Dock 18 tonight and see what we see. Don't worry," he adds. "This Skeet is probably just full of hot air."

"Come on," Tina urges. "Aren't you curious? We won't let anything happen to you."

You look at Randy and then at Tina. Their faces shine with eagerness. You sigh.

"Let me think about it," you tell them.

* * *

You decide to talk it over with Satellite Jack. He may be eccentric, but he's smart and he's not reckless. He could probably also convince Randy and Tina that backing out of this little adventure doesn't make you a chicken!

You find Satellite Jack at lunch time. You spot him sitting on a bench under a tree in the schoolyard. He holds an apple with a bite taken out of it in one hand. You ask him breathlessly if he got your e-mail this morning.

Jack doesn't respond. His head is cocked to one side, staring at absolutely nothing, his eyes glassy. The hand with the apple doesn't move. He gets this way sometimes. It's like he's tuned into some frequency from outer space.

Suddenly he's startled to see you. "Uh, sorry, I was on another wavelength. What'd you say?"

You explain again about the messages from Skeet99 this morning and tell him about Randy and Tina's crazy plan to go down to the dock tonight.

"Huh." He squints at the apple as if surprised to find it in his hand. He takes a bite and crunches slowly. "Scientists used to think that disease was caused by vapors, humors, and ill winds. Then when the microscope was invented, they found it was really caused by all these tiny invisible bugs."

"Yeah... so?" Sometimes Jack's logic is a little far out for you to follow.

"What I'm saying is that you can wonder what this message means until your head explodes, but you won't get anywhere until you get a closer look at the real source of the problem."

Uh oh. That sounds suspiciously as if Jack agrees with Randy and Tina.

"Can't the police do that?" Even as you ask the question, you know the answer. No real crime has been committed. They won't be interested.

Jack slaps your knee. "Let's do it! Of course, I mean us in the broadest sense," he adds hastily. "I won't be going down there myself. I'll stay in the control center and monitor communications. If it gets hairy, I'll dial 911."

"Wait a minute control center, communications, *what?*" As usual, Jack is making your head spin.

"I've got all the equipment, see? All this stuff I've been working on, we can use it for the investigation. I didn't invent it for nothing!"

Your eyes widen as his face lights up. You thought Jack would be more reasonable than Randy and Tina. Instead, he's talking so fast you're not sure how he can breathe.

"The first thing you'll need is my MicroJack," he declares. "It's kind of like a handheld computer with rocket engines. You can use it for voice mail, e-mail, and a lot of other stuff. Plus, I've been working on this portable scanner...and a digital camera..."

Jack bounces up and down on the bench with each device

he names. When Satellite Jack gets excited, there's no way to stop him. It's like a big snowball rolling downhill, picking up mass and momentum. And you're right in its path.

"Stop!" you exclaim.

Jack takes another big bite into the apple. "What?" he mumbles through a mushy mouthful. "You don't want to do it?"

You take a moment to think. And decide that, as scary as it is, you *do* want to do this. So, you go for a change of subject. "No," you tell Jack. "I think there's a worm in your apple!"

Jack peers at the fruit, frowns at the brown track running through its center, then shrugs. "Extra protein." He tosses the apple into a garbage can and stands up to leave. "Let's meet after school. At the park. You tell Tina, I'll tell Randy. It's time for action."

*　　*　　*

There's a little town park between school and your house where the four of you often meet. You sit on a concrete picnic table under a swaying eucalyptus. Jack tosses a bag of corn chips onto the table. You all begin to scarf down the snacks while you talk.

It's been decided. You're going to investigate the mysterious e-mail messages from Skeet99 and whatever else might be going on down on the waterfront. You're still a little nervous because it's your neck on the line—you're the one who's the target of the threatening messages. But you know Randy, Tina and Jack will stick by you. Plus, you have to admit it feels good to take action of some kind rather than waiting around for something to happen to you—no matter how creepy the docks at night might be.

"We'll conduct this investigation like real detectives," Tina declares.

"Excellent." Jack crunches a handful of chips. "We'll call ourselves the Digital Detectives," he announces, licking salt from his fingers. He grins. "I've been saving the name for a long time."

You look at Tina, who looks at Randy, who looks back at you. "Sounds good to me," you say. The others nod.

"Digital Detectives, at your service," Randy pronounces. He thumps you on the back. "You're our first client."

"Hey, I'm an investigator too," you remind him.

"Oh, so now you *want* to head down to the North End," Tina teases. The North End is the industrial waterfront part of town, where Dock 18 is located.

"Of course," you state firmly. "In fact, since I'm personally involved, I'll take the lead in this case."

Jack passes around the bag of chips. "Okay, let me tell you about some of the equipment I'll have for you tonight. First of all, there's the handheld scanner. I believe I'll call it the JackScan. Yes?"

You all shake your heads. Jack sometimes has to be reminded not to get too full of himself. But as often happens, the reminder goes right by him.

"Good, the JackScan," he continues. "It's small, about the size of a flashlight, but it can record any pattern you see. That includes handwriting, printed matter, footprints, tire tracks, blood spatters....Fingerprints, too, if you use dust first to bring out the print."

Jack never ceases to amaze you. You know better than to ask how he can afford the components for his inventions. Tina did once, and Jack answered loftily, "I've got *patents*, my dear."

It might even be true that he's registered some of his inventions with the patent office. He *is* a genius, after all. But it's also true that before they moved to Crescent Bay, his parents made a fortune in the early days of Silicon Valley. They seem happy to provide him with whatever he needs, and he puts what they give him to good use.

"Second," Jack continues, "there's the digital camera. You all probably know how to use it. This one, though, has a sort of periscope attachment that will allow you to take pictures around a corner."

"Cool," Tina says, munching chips. She hands you the bag.

Jack's eyes glitter as he finishes listing the goodies he has in store for you. "Finally, best of all, you'll have the MicroJack. It will store and organize all of the data you collect, allowing you to catalogue and compare clues. It's like a virtual crime lab that you can carry wherever you go. Not only that, it's got wireless access to the Internet. We can e-mail each other and keep in touch by voice. It's a phenomenal piece of technology, if I do say so myself."

"You're great, Jack." Randy's admiration is genuine. "That equipment sounds amazing. But there are probably a few low tech tools we should all bring too. A flashlight. A magnifying glass. A pair of binoculars."

"Right," you agree. You take a chip and hand the bag back to Jack.

"Are you sure you don't want to come to the dock with us,

Jack?" Tina asks. "You're going to miss all the action."

Jack glances down at the corn chip in his hand, then tosses it to a squirrel. "Naw, someone has to hold down the fort."

Jack slides down off the picnic table. "I'd better get home now. I need to fine tune your equipment for tonight." He wipes his salty fingers on the seat of his pants. "All detectives meet in the North End," he orders. "Behind Fanelli's gas station, at 10:00 p.m."

Jack trundles off into the park. The rest of you start figuring out how to slip out of your houses tonight. After all, if your parents catch you sneaking out, your punishment could quite possibly be worse than anything Skeet can do.

At least, that's what you hope.

∃
DOCK 18

Your parents never suspect a thing. You don't do it a lot, but you've snuck out of your house before. You've got the technique down.

It's important to start early. A big open-jawed yawn right after dessert kicks it off. You cover your mouth with your hand just before your mom tells you to. You make sure you spend a little time in the living room, where your parents are watching some lawyer show on TV. Lying down to watch for a few minutes, you allow your eyes to flutter closed and remain motionless for several minutes. Then you sit up with a start, as if suddenly waking. You rub your eyes, yawn some more, and around nine o'clock you tell your parents good night.

You stumble upstairs to your bedroom, and quickly check the computer. No more messages from Skeet. That's good. You crawl into bed, fully dressed. You force yourself to lie still in the dark for half an hour. Then you climb out of bed and replace your sleeping form with some old stuffed animals. You grab your jacket and slip out the window.

Luckily, your bedroom window looks out on the roof of the front porch. The roof isn't too steep, and you can tiptoe across it to a tree that is easy to climb down. You keep low as you run to the end of the house, then turn and follow a hedge out to a bush where you've hidden your bike. Then you're off down the street heading toward the North End.

Crescent Bay got its name from a long sweeping beach that runs three miles along the water in the curving shape of a crescent moon. This is the crescent that forms the bay and protects the town from the pounding swells of the Pacific. It makes for some nice surfing waves, and a good place for boats to anchor.

At the north end, in the last curl of the crescent just before rocky cliffs rise to close off the bay, is a flat area that used to be a salt water marsh. The town's fishing industry first started here, and the marsh has become a marine-industrial district, home to small fish processing and canning operations, boat yards, metal shops, and warehouses. Even though a few dot-com startup companies have moved in recently, the fishing industry still does business at the docks and wharves of the North End.

Fanelli's gas station is on Pacific Boulevard, the four lane street that divides the residential neighborhoods from the industrial North End. You find the rest of the Digital Detectives in a weedy vacant lot behind the station. They're ready to go.

Jack gives each of you a pack containing your investigative tools. "You might want to test them out first," he advises. "Although, I know for a fact that they all work like a breeze."

You thank him and strap the pack on your back. He glances around nervously. "Well, I better get back home so I can monitor the operation. Good luck."

Tina and Randy lock their bikes with yours. You look at one another, take a deep breath, then set off on foot for Dock 18.

Randy has scouted it out. It's about eight blocks down through the deserted, oil soaked streets of the North End.

Here and there a lone street lamp lights the low hulking warehouses and razor-wire fences. A buoy clangs in the distance. It reminds you of sunny days out on the bay, in the sun, on a surfboard, when you didn't have a care in the world, aside from getting creamed by a wave. A pair of squawking gulls flies overhead, in search of scraps left behind by the fish processing operations. You shiver. This place has a little too much atmosphere, you think to yourself.

You're within a block of your destination, when two sharp cracks break the night.

"What was that?" you gasp.

"A BB gun," Randy says. He yanks you and Tina into the shadows. You hear raised voices, then gunning engines. Tires squeal, and a dark blue pickup truck comes racing around the corner and down the street. A moment later, you hear the sound of two motorcycle engines. They peel out, but you only catch the flash of their headlights.

The sound of the engines recedes in the distance. Then, all is quiet again. All except the pounding of your heart.

The quiet is eerie after that outburst. Crouched in the shadow of a brick warehouse, you trade glances with Tina and Randy. Without speaking, you know they're thinking the same thing you are: the e-mail from Skeet99 was no joke. There's something going on tonight at Dock 18. Something dangerous.

"Let's give it a couple more minutes," Randy whispers. "Just to make sure they're gone."

Tina pulls her sleeve back from her watch. After exactly two minutes she says impatiently, "All right, let's go."

Keeping to the shadows, the three of you creep down the block. The dock and a few small buildings are dimly outlined against the void beyond, the black water of the bay

The gate to Dock 18 has been left open. You enter it slowly, cautiously, your ears pricked for the slightest sound. Nothing stirs except the dust, caught in the yellow of a distant harbor light, speckling the air from the hasty departure of the vehicles.

You look at Tina, then Randy. "Let's begin this investigation," you declare.

Begin your investigation on
the Digital Detectives web site:
http://www.ddmysteries.com
and enter the key phrase **DOCK18**

When you've finished this investigation,
the web site will give you a page number
to return to.

You leave Dock 18 and begin to head back to your bikes. As you walk, you review the evidence you found there with Randy and Tina.

"I don't know," Tina says, doubt in her voice. "I have a feeling there was more there we could have found."

"Yeah," Randy agrees. "There were a few places that we might have missed."

You look at him, then at Tina. "Really? Are you sure you want to go back?"

"We came all the way out here," Tina reasons. "We might as well do the job right."

You want nothing more than to escape while your skin is still intact. But one glance at Randy lets you know that he thinks you should go back, too.

You stop. "Okay," you say, turning back toward the dock. "Let's go finish the job."

Return to the Digital Detectives web site to do some more investigation:

http://www.ddmysteries.com

and enter the key phrase **LEFTDOCK**

When you've finished this investigation, the web site will give you a page number to return to.

"Let go of me!" you shout at the guy who has you pinned to the ground at Dock 18. You glance over and see that Tina and Randy are also flat on their backs, struggling against a pair of thuggish looking teens.

"Who are you guys?" you demand. Man, his grip is tight, you think.

"Funny, that was *my* question," the guy with the steel-like fingers replies.

"We're not doing anything," Randy insists. "We were just looking around."

He shakes a CD disk at you. "What's this doing here, then?"

"We don't know anything about it," Tina says, returning his anger. "We heard some guy named Skeet was up to something down here, so we came to check it out."

"Skeet, huh? Well, tell Skeet and his pal Travis that we don't like them moving in on our market."

"Market for what?" you ask.

The guy practically plasters the disk into your face. "What are you, stupid? Look, if you know what's good for you, you'll keep your faces out of our business."

The guy gives Randy a little slap in the face, then stands up. With that, the rest of them get up off you. They stomp away back to their motorcycles, gun the engines threateningly, and roar off into the night.

The three of you get up and dust yourselves off.
"Nice guys," Randy says.

"They think they're tough," Tina states. "But they can't scare me. Let's get back to our investigation."

"Yeah, I don't think we found everything yet," Randy agrees.

You take a deep breath. "All right. Let's just keep our ears open, okay?"

Return to the Digital Detectives web site to continue your investigation:

http://www.ddmysteries.com

and enter the key phrase **CAPTURED**

When you've finished this investigation, the web site will give you a page number to return to.

You agree with Randy. "Yeah, let's go before someone else comes along and bothers us."

Tina and Randy help you pack up your investigation tools. You slip through the Dock 18 fence and race back to your bikes. Suddenly, the blue pickup truck comes careening around a corner. It catches you in its headlights for a moment, just before you can go down a narrow passage between two buildings and duck with Randy and Tina. The truck screeches to a stop. But you're able to run down to the next block and lose it again.

"I think they saw us," you say breathlessly.

"Let's just get back to our bikes," Tina says, dashing ahead.

Once you get back to the gas station and unlock your bikes, you feel a little safer. Suddenly, it dawns on you that you've pulled off your mission.

"We did it!" you burst out to your friends.

"Yeah, and we found some pretty interesting stuff," Tina agrees.

You exchange grins and hand slaps with her and Randy. Then you jump on your bikes to head home.

4
THE AVENGING BEETLE

Everyone is talking at once. It's lunch time and the Digital Detectives have gathered at a table in the corner of the school cafeteria. You glance around. You don't want anyone to overhear you as you review the results of your investigation last night.

Satellite Jack pounds the table. "Everyone! Quiet!"
You all shut up at once. Jack has that effect on people.
Satisfied that he has your attention, Jack continues. "This has to be an orderly process! We need to review the pieces of evidence one by one, like a compiler in a computer. Now, since I didn't get to go last night, I'll..."

"*Get* to go? We practically got killed," Tina interrupts.

"It wasn't that bad," Randy protests.

"Jack's right," you say. "We have to analyze this stuff piece by piece."

"Thank you." He pushes his food tray aside to make room for his briefcase. Jack's one of the few kids you know who carries a briefcase, and one of the few who can get away with it. He pulls out a laptop computer and opens it up.

"Now, I've compiled it all into a database" Jack says. "Let's start with the fingerprints, footprints, and tire tracks."

You stare at him. He is unbelievably organized.

"We got a bunch," you say. "But we don't know who they belong to."

"Of course not," Tina replies. "This is just the first step. You look for more. Then we can start comparing them to each other, when we know who our suspects are."

You heave a big sigh, causing everyone to wait for you to speak. "Well, there's some guy named Travis. All I can say is, I'm glad we found out those e-mail messages weren't for me."

"Yeah, that was good," Tina agrees. "See? One mystery solved already. But let's not talk about suspects til the end, after we've reviewed all the clues."

"Exactly." Jack punches up a new screen. "Next we've got physical and visual evidence. The piece of flannel fabric. The eyeglass lens. The INSECT INVADERS disk. The beetles."

"Dead bugs. What can they tell us?" Tina demands.

A smirk comes across Jack's face. You can tell he's about to deliver one of his zingers. "A lot. I researched it this morning. That particular beetle doesn't live in this area. The closest place it can be found is Mexico."

"Oh," Tina says. "So how'd it get all the way up here? That's the question."

"Yep," Randy affirms. "Maybe it has something to do with that yacht we saw out on the water. *Sweet* something; did anyone see the whole name?"

You and Tina shake your heads.

"Okay," Jack says. "I think that covers most of those clues. Now let's review the written and verbal clues."

"There's that code key we found in the drawer," you point out. "Don't ask me what it decodes, but we've got it."

"There was a computer game magazine in the shack, too," Randy says. "It was open to a review of INSECT

INVADERS—said it was the gooeyest game ever made."

"Must be true," Tina observes. "Jason's stuck to it like a fly on flypaper."

"Plus there's the receipt from Walter's store." Randy turns and looks at Jack. "You don't think Walter's mixed up in this, do you?"

Old Walter runs a store that sells used CDs, tapes, and computer games down on Branch Avenue. You've been there a few times and always find cool stuff cheap. He and Jack are kind of friends.

Jack taps the edge of his computer thoughtfully. At the moment, with his plump lips slightly parted and tight brown curls framing his apple cheeks, he looks like an anxious cherub.

Jack pushes his glasses up on his nose and exhales slowly. "Yeah, I guess that makes Walter a suspect. Let's start the list." He types in Walter's name and asks, "Who else?"

"Travis," you say. "And Skeet99, whoever he is."

"They mentioned a warehouse. Maybe Skeet's involved with that," Tina offers.

"What I want to know is, who's Annie?" you add. "The e-mail made it sound like everything counted on her. Maybe she's the master mind."

"Yeah, but of what?" Tina demands.

"Oh, come on," Jack responds. "You guys have figured it out by now, don't you?" Jack spreads his palms on the table. The angelic look is gone. Now he's puffed up like one of those funny looking gargoyles, which you've seen on buildings.

"All right," he declares. He ticks off the clues on his fingers.

"You've got INSECT INVADERS in the magazine. You've got a few copies of the game disk, still shrink-wrapped, in a carton, along with some beetles from Mexico. You've got the guys on the motorcycles, who are rivals of Travis and Skeet. What does that add up to?"

"A computer game piracy ring," you say.

Jack points at you. "Ding ding ding! Right answer. The disks are copied in Mexico. They're shipped here to be distributed up and down the coast." He taps the computer again. "But it must be a new operation, or the other pirates wouldn't have been down there trying to scare them off."

"Let's suppose you're right..." Randy begins.

"Oh, I'm right," Jack insists.

Before you can jump all over Jack's ego, a voice interrupts the conversation. "You guys playing a computer game?"
Jason the Destroyer stands a few feet away. He's holding a lunch tray and peering with a kind of cockeyed expression at Jack's laptop.

Your heads swivel in unison. As you look at him, you realize the reason his face looks crooked is that the right lens is missing from his glasses. A lens exactly the shape of the one you found at the dock.

The four of you fall silent. Finally Tina gives him a weak smile. "Hey, Jason. No, it's just some school stuff."

"Oh." Jason squints at you through his one good lens. "Later," he says and goes to find another table.

All eyes are on Tina. She's pretty good at hiding her surprise, though. In a very calm voice she says, "I guess we need to add Jason to the suspect list."

* * *

After school, you and Jack head to Walter's Recycling, down on Branch Avenue, the main shopping street in Crescent Bay.

By the end of lunch, you have divided up duties for investigating the computer game piracy ring—if that's what it is. Tina insisted on calling it a "theory" until more evidence is found. It was decided that you and Jack would check out Walter's store. Tina would go and have a talk with Jason, while Randy would try to find out who Travis is.

Walter's Recycling is a cluttered place. The high ceilings are gray with dust and all the little nooks of the shop are packed with racks of used CDs, audio tapes, video tapes, video game cartridges, and computer games. The one place that's dusted and clean as a whistle is the corner where Old Walter keeps his LP records, most of them are from the 50s, 60s, and 70s. Jack told you Old Walter used to be a radio DJ.

Jack got friendly with Walter because he was always in the store looking for music he could sample from. You were amazed to find out that one of Jack's favorite things to do, when he's not inventing new devices, is to use his computers to mix music. You wonder how many other surprises Jack has up his sleeves.

Old Walter gives Jack his usual gruff, hearty greeting when you come in the door. "My man Jack, he's back, come to rake over the racks."

Walter's way of talking is fun to listen to. Walter himself has a bit of a bulge over his belt, usually covered by an olive-green button down sweater. His arthritis kind of slows him down, but every once in a while he'll pop a dance move to let you know he's still got it.

Jack mumbles a greeting in return. You can tell it troubles him to be here as part of an investigation. The two of you saunter down the aisles. Walter goes back to logging in a stack of CD's sitting on the counter.

Pretty soon you find it. A whole row of INSECT INVADERS disks in the computer games section. You show them to Jack and his shoulders sag. "Keep looking," he whispers. "I'll talk to Walter."

Jack goes up to the front counter. "So, Walter, how's business?"

"Busy-ness is not too busy, Jack. They just opened that new computer store down the street. You've been there, I'm sure."

"You mean Wham!? Sure, I checked it out."

"You and everybody else. All that you kids want to spend your money on is computer games. INSECT INVADERS. It's taking over the world."

Jack folds his arms and leans against the counter. "Uh, yeah...I noticed you have some copies of the game back there."

"Yeah, tryin' to keep up."

"A pretty good price too—80% off, it looks like."

"Something like that. It's a darned expensive game. I don't know how they get away with charging that much."

"And yours are still in their shrink wrapping."

As they talk, you're busy dusting the shrink wrap on a couple of disks and scanning in fingerprints. You feel kind of sneaky, but you also feel excited, like a real detective.

"Yeah." Walter peers over his reading glasses at Jack. "What's with the questions, you working for the IRS now?"

Jack gives a short laugh. "No, uh...well, I was just wondering where you got them."

"I guess that's none of your business, is it Jack?"

You look up to see Jack recoil a little. Walter goes back to his paperwork, then adds, "But since you're a good customer, I'll tell you. Besides, I'm curious about something myself."

Walter stops, removes his glasses, and lets them hang from a chain around his neck. "You know, I don't care much for these games. Why do kids want to spend all their time staring at some computer screen, when they could be playing and having fun with other kids? Can you explain that to me? Why do you all cut yourselves off from each other and twiddle your thumbs on these games?"

Jack seems to be shrinking before your eyes. "I don't really know," he stammers. "I don't play them much, myself."

You open your mouth to speak up and help Jack out. You're not sure what you're going to say, but you're interrupted by the jangle of the front door before you have to actually speak. A man steps in and the door slams shut behind him.

Walter glares at him. "What about you, Bughead? Can you explain it? What's so fascinating about these games? Like that new one—INSECT INVADERS?"

The man stops and shifts from foot to foot. You've seen him before. He's in his late twenties and wears a flannel shirt under a threadbare corduroy jacket. His tousled hair sticks out all over the place and he's got a couple of days growth on his face.

You know he must have a real name, but everyone in town calls him Bug Man. He's totally into scarabs, which is a special kind of Egyptian beetle. He has a purple tattoo of a scarab on his neck and sports a giant scarab belt buckle.

Bug Man looks at Walter, narrows his eyes, and repeats "INSECT INVADERS" slowly, drawing out the words with scorn. He raises two fingers and jabs them like a fork at an imaginary figure in front of him, as if putting out its eyes.

"Right on," says Walter.

Bug Man drops his arm. "They owe me a lot of money, man," he says in a perfectly normal voice.

"Why's that?" Walter asks.

Bug Man flings open his jacket and points at the belt buckle. "They stole the whole idea from me! I met with the CEO...what's her name, Sandra Cye...two years ago. Now look at them, making millions, like little grubs hatching under a log."

Walter grunts. You have a feeling he's heard this rant before. But Bug Man has got your and Jack's attention.

"The power of the scarab cannot be corrupted," he goes on. "Vengeance will rain down upon them. Mark my words, by the great Anubis, all the plagues of the pharaohs shall visit their houses. Unless they render unto the scarab that which is the scarab's."

"Which is...?" Jack asks.

"Royalties! Tribute to the Great Insect." Bug Man pounds his belt buckle so hard you're afraid he's going to hurt himself. "Offerings to his Highness of Six Legs."

Walter just smiles and shakes his head. "You should go down the street and talk to those protesters at that new store, Arthur. They're all..."

"Someone's protesting the game?" you blurt. This is news!

Walter nods. "Yeah, right down there at the Wham! Go see for yourself. A bunch of parents, I think. They've sure got a beef with INSECT INVADERS."

"They are misguided," Bug Man says darkly. "We must not resist the Insect."

You exchange looks with Jack, and you can tell he's thinking the same thing as you: some interesting information to check out here.

Walter puts his glasses back on and returns to his paperwork. Meanwhile, Bug Man zeroes in on Jack again. He launches into a monologue about the mystical powers of the scarab and how it rules over both life, death, and rebirth, which has something to do with the fact that it grows out of animal dung.

While Jack listens politely, you take the digital camera from your pack and manage to sneak a couple pictures of Bug Man.

You stuff the camera back in your pack, then sidle up to the counter with a copy of the game. You try to sound casual as you ask Walter, "So...where'd you say you got these?"

"What's it say on the back?" Walter demands.

You read the copy on the back of the disk.

The human race had its chance. Now it's their turn. Mutant insects have gained the power of intelligence. They're too fast for guns. Pesticides only make them stronger.
One person stands between them and World Domination. And there's only one way to stop them....Eat or be eaten.

Walter frowns. "No, not *that*. The name of the company that made it."

"Oh. It was made by TerrorStruck Games. A division of Cye-Tek."

"Right. That's who sold it to me. Some guy came in with a box and said that they printed the labels wrong or something. They were unloading them cheap."

"Um, was his name Travis by any chance?"

"Don't know. Never got a name. He had hair that was short in front, long in the back. Young—maybe even high school age, come to think of it."

You want to ask Walter if he really believes the guy worked for Cye-Tek, but you can't quite get up the nerve. Walter eyes the INSECT INVADERS disk you're turning over and over in your hand.

"You going to buy that?" he says abruptly.

"Uh, no." You lay the game on the counter. "No, I don't really need it."

"Good," says Walter.

* * *

You and Jack leave Walter's store and head down Branch Avenue toward Wham! You see the protesters marching back and forth in the parking lot in front of the store, from across the street.

Jack starts to cross the street. "Whoa!" you yelp, throwing your arm out to stop him. A blue pickup truck is coming straight for him.

"I think that's the truck from Dock 18," you whisper

urgently. "Look away."

You and Jack turn your backs and pretend to be talking about something, while the truck passes slowly. When you turn back, there's a break in the traffic. You cross the street quickly.

"Do you think they saw us?" Jack asks.

"Maybe," you answer in a worried voice as you peer down the street. "They're turning around and coming back this way."

You and Jack quickly make your way through the parking lot to the entrance of the store, where a bunch of adults are gathering. Out of the corner of your eye, you see the blue pickup truck turn into the lot.

The adults near the door are marching back and forth in front of the store. They carry signs that say things like:

CYE-TEK—OUT OF MY CHILD'S BRAIN! KEEP YOUR FEELERS OFF MY KID!

As the protesters pace in an orderly circle, they chant, "Stop the invasion! Stamp out the pests!"

It's not too hard to get them to tell you what they're all about. As you approach, a woman sitting at a card table covered with flyers calls out to you. "Hi, kids!" she says brightly.

"Hi," you say.

"Do you kids play computer games?" she asks in a syrupy voice.

"No, not us, ma'am," you reply.

"Unless you call hacking the backbone server for the North American Air Defense Command a computer game," Jack says in a perfectly serious tone.

The woman's smile remains frozen on her face. She takes a breath and says, "Well, we're encouraging kids to read books, play tennis, join the school band, that sort of thing. Instead of wasting their minds on the, what do you call them, twitching games this company sells."

You and Jack stifle a laugh. "Twitch," Jack corrects her.

An earnest fellow in a blue dress shirt joins you. He tries a different approach. "Look, I understand the appeal of this game, I really do." He winks. "I killed some bugs in my day. It's all good fun. But I was out in the sunshine, in the real world." "Wow," you want to say. "That's macho." But you just smile.

"You know what really *bugs* me?" The guy laughs at his own lame joke. "What bugs me is how much money the company is making off it. They charge sixty dollars! Isn't that outrageous? Think of all the other things you could do with sixty dollars."

"You can get the bootleg version for about ten," Jack says.

This stops the guy cold. Then, his eyes light up as he sees someone coming out of the store. You recognize the man too.

"Mr. Purdue!" you exclaim.

Kyle Purdue runs the computer lab at school. He's carrying a cardboard box and is dressed in his usual outfit: khaki pants and a blue-jean work shirt. You and Jack see him just about every day, but he takes a step back when he notices you. "Oh, hi there."

"Are you here protesting the game?" you ask.

"No, no, it's uh...well, of course, I support their right to free speech." He gives a confused look to the two adults at the table. "Okay, see you later," he says. He turns around and goes right back into the store.

You grab a couple of flyers from the table, thank the man and woman, and head off. "You're welcome!" the woman calls after you cheerfully.

"Stop the Insect Child Killers," Jack reads. "SICK. That's what the group is called."

For the second time in an hour, you throw your arm out to halt Jack in his tracks. "What now?" he complains.

You nudge his shoulder in the direction you're looking. The blue pickup truck is parked in the next row down in the lot, facing the store.

"Let's check it out," you say. "I've got a funny feeling about this truck."

Jack resists your tug on his sleeve. "I don't know..."

"Come on, the driver's probably in the store."

You half-drag Jack to take a closer look at the truck. It's brand spanking new, midnight blue, with chrome wheels and a big camper shell on the back. Everything on the truck bulges, as if it's on steroids.

You crane your neck to get a look inside. The windows are tinted, so it's hard to see anything.

You've just about reached the front bumper of the truck, when you freeze. "I think someone's in there!"

Suddenly, both doors to the truck burst open. You don't pause to look, you just grab Jack and run for it.

"Yaaaaa!" Jack screams.

Behind you, you hear the doors slam and the engine roar to life.

5
THE YELLOW EYES

You race down the sidewalk to escape the blue pickup truck. Jack lags behind, and you have to force yourself to slow down to wait for him. It's not easy; your insides are a jumble of panic, and your legs shake with the urge to run as fast and as far as you can.

The truck screeches to a stop at the parking lot exit. You've caught a break. The truck has to wait for traffic.

"Come on!" you cry. Desperately you scan the street for a place to hide.

"There!" you say, pointing to a fast food joint across the street. You yank Jack's arm and dart through traffic, just as the pickup peels out of the parking lot.

You burst through the doors of the restaurant. You feel everyone staring at you, as you race to the far end and duck down behind a planter.

Jack jerks his arm away from you. "Let go already."

The two of you slump to the floor, exhausted. You lean against the planter. Jack is gasping. Sweat trickles down the side of his plump face. "Do you think we're safe?"

"Safe from what?" someone says above you.

You look up to see a kid, whom you know from school. He's holding a broom and is wearing an apron stamped with the name of the joint: All In Bun.

41

"Some creep in a blue pickup truck was chasing us," you answer.

The kid saunters over to the window. He comes back a minute later and announces, "No blue pickup truck out there."

You peer cautiously over the planter. You didn't get a look at the driver of the truck, but the customers, standing in line to order, look harmless enough.

"Okay, thanks," you say to the kid.

As you brush yourself off, Jack wipes his glasses. "I seriously need a hot dog, okay?"

You keep glancing from side to side, as you get in line, expecting a big hairy hand to grab you at any moment. But you manage to get your order and sit down without any more trouble.

Jack seems to have recovered. He regards his hot dog as if it were a work of art, which it almost is. The wiener is buried under a composition of colors drawn from just about every item in the condiment bin: green relish, red ketchup, yellow mustard, and white onions, to name a few.

You're just starting to relax yourself, biting into a chili dog, when a teenage girl strides over to you. She's got dyed, teased auburn hair, cherry lips, and about the meanest eyes you've ever seen.

"We know who you are," she says, stabbing a long purple-nailed finger at the middle of your face. "And you better keep your little noses out of our business."

She marches out the door, leaving behind a whiff of perfume that pretty much ruins your appetite.

* * *

You don't want to go out your door alone the next morning. You barely slept last night. You couldn't stop thinking. About the pickup truck and its tinted windows. About the shiny purple fingernail in your face. About the fact that they know who you are.

At first it had been exciting to call Tina and Randy and tell them about your narrow escape. But then, as the night grew darker outside, you paced the house nervously. You couldn't concentrate on your homework. Again and again you checked through the windows for the midnight blue truck.

The worst thing was, you couldn't tell your family about it. Your mom would be very, very disappointed if you had to explain how you snuck out of the house to go down to the dock.

But they definitely sensed something was up. She asked you if anything was wrong and you said no, you were just trying to figure out how to write an English essay. Eve, your little sister, picked up on it, too. She asked if you wanted to play a game on the computer. You know she was just trying to cheer you up, but you said no. You didn't want to tempt yourself to check your e-mail, in case you found another message from Skeet99.

You feel a little better now that it's morning. Still, you wait at the window for Randy to come out his door. As soon as you see him, you dash out to join him. Even with him at your side, you keep glancing all around you.

"Looking for that truck, huh?" he asks.

You nod, but don't say anything. Does he think you're a chicken?

"It's pretty creepy, all right," he says. "You don't think they know where you live, do you?"

"I hope not." You try to keep your voice steady.

As you turn the corner, you see Tina waiting for you up the block, rocking impatiently on her skateboard. She makes a few turns down the sidewalk to join you.

"Hey," Randy says, "I asked my brother about that girl, who pointed her finger at you, at the All In Bun. He said it sounded like a girl in his high school. Her name's Tammy."

"Tammy," Tina snorts. "Let her try pointing one of those claws at *me*. I'll give her a new manicure."

"You guys," you blurt. "Don't you think maybe we should call the cops?"

Tina scowls. "No! It's just starting to get interesting."

"Well, you're not the one they're following!"

Tina shakes her head. "Believe me, it won't do us any good. They're not going to take some kids seriously, when all we can tell them is that someone *might* be following you and that some girl pointed at you. We need more. They've got too much other stuff to do."

Tina's words carry a lot of weight because her father works with the police department. He's a paramedic, but sometimes he helps out the County Medical Examiner. You think her dad is cool. He's a quiet guy, but he loves the outdoors and is full of interesting information about everything from the latest police case to what kind of plankton whales like to eat.

Randy nods, and you have to agree, that if you went into the police station and told them only what you know so far, you might end up feeling kind of silly.

"Besides," Tina says, "it's more fun to solve the case ourselves. We're the Digital Detectives, remember?"

Randy puts his hand on your shoulder. "And we're in this together."

You take a deep breath. "Right." You force yourself to think about the investigation, instead of worrying about getting ambushed by Travis. "So...that's pretty weird about Jason, huh? Do you really think he might be involved?"

Last night, Tina had told you about her visit to Jason the Destroyer's house. She showed him the missing lens. He grabbed it and fit it back into his glasses. But he denied being at Dock 18. He claimed he lost the lens when he fell off his bike and didn't know how it ended up down there.

Tina also said Jason was really distracted. All he could talk about was finding the secret level in INSECT INVADERS. He didn't really seem to care that she was asking him all those questions. He just wanted to play the game. On her way out, Tina snuck into Jason's garage to scan the tire treads on his bike. She felt bad, gathering evidence on a friend like that, but it was her job, as a Digital Detective.

"You guys haven't heard the latest," Tina says. "Jason called me again last night, all upset. His computer melted down."

"Hmm," you respond. "That's too bad, but it happens."

"Yeah, but it happened while he was playing the game. He found the secret level. He said it was in the larva squashing scene. He took this one larva and let it hatch and it spun into the secret level. Then...meltdown."

"Do you think they might be connected?" Randy asks.

Tina pulls something from out of the big orange and black messenger bag, which she keeps strapped over her shoulder. It's the game disk you found at the dock. "I think we ought to check it out. See if there's something different about this disk. Jack thinks so, too. He's waiting for us in the computer lab, so let's move it!"

*   *   *

You know what Satellite Jack has planned for you as you come down the hallway with Tina. Only someone who knows Jack well would know to look for the tiny microphone taped near the front door to the computer lab. You spot it right away. Jack will be inside monitoring the sound, which the mike feeds him. He will have heard your voices, as you approach.

Sure enough, the back door swings open just as you reach it. "I've been expecting you," Jack intones with arched brows.

He quickly shuts the door behind you. You don't ask how Jack can get into the computer lab in the mornings before it opens, and Jack doesn't tell. He just takes the game disk from Tina and inserts it into the drive of a computer, which he's already got booted. It's the fastest machine in the lab, naturally.

"Where's Randy?" he asks.

"He had a soccer team meeting," Tina says.

Jack's eyes never leave the screen. He doesn't bother to play the game, just somehow gets access to pages of code that take him to the screen he wants.

"Ahh, the legendary larva stomping scene," he says.

"Hurry, they're starting to hatch!" Tina tells him.

Jack points to his headphones. "Someone's coming. Make sure the door's locked."

A moment later, a knock comes at the door. Tina starts to turn the lock, but then opens it when she hears the voice behind it. "It's me, Jason."

"I asked him to come," Tina explains to you and Jack.

She locks the door behind Jason. You give him a nod, then turn your attention back to the screen, where Jack is squashing a few larvae just for fun. Splat! Green pudding squirts out of them.

"You're going to have to eat all of that, you know," Jason warns.

"Which one goes to the secret level?" Jack demands.

"It's got red and yellow stripes," Jason says. "In the back, on the left. Yeah, that's it. Okay, now keep clicking it, fast. It'll spin a bunch of thread—like that. Just let it do it. Okay, now you're in the new level. The lair."

You find yourself holding your breath. Jack's avatar is in some underground interior space with fleshy, pinkish walls. Cobweb strands snake down from the ceiling, swaying in time to the deep thrum of a heartbeat. After a moment, you realize the moist looking walls are throbbing too, very slowly, slightly out of sync with the heartbeat. For some reason, their deliberate, barely visible ebb is more threatening than anything else there.

You jump when a tarantula comes shrieking in from behind a cobweb. Jack's avatar loses an arm.

"You gotta be fast," Jason says.

"Forget that," Jack answers. "I'm going to crack this thing before I lose any more limbs."

Jack hits some combinations on the keyboard. Nothing happens. He waits. A tiny insect spins down on a strand from the ceiling above Jack.

"Brown mite," Jason warns. "It's poisonous."

Jack moves, but too late. There's a shout of pain, then a blood-red dot on the avatar's neck. It begins to pulse and grow.

Jack sets his jaw and glares at the screen. He slams a few more keys, but he can't escape. You spot a bristling leg feeling its way out from a fleshy fold in the wall.

"Look out! On the left!" you cry.

But it's too late. There goes Jack's other arm.

He sits back, stares at the screen, and clamps his teeth down on his thumb.

Something changes in the scene. You can't tell what it is at first. Then you realize the throbs in the walls have grown larger. Small networks of red veins appear on their swelling surfaces.

"Oh no," Jason breathes.

The throbs become more pronounced. It seems with each pulse the reddening walls will burst. And then they do—or no, they don't burst, but instead turn inside out, releasing thousands of spiders hidden in their folds. The creatures swarm over the screen. It's nothing but a mass of writhing black legs. The head of one giant tarantula emerges from the mass to fix its yellow eyes on you. It comes closer and closer, coming to swallow you up. The yellow eyes fill the screen. They melt into a lurid, fiendish face, its features twisting as it laughs demonically.

"Kiss your hard drive good bye," Jason intones.

A hollow voice croaks the exact same words from the computer. The screen turns a dead green muck color that you've never seen before.

Jack gapes at the computer. You've never seen him so dumbfounded.

"Revenge of the insects," Tina tries to joke. But Jack doesn't move a muscle.

"Four thousand dollars," he says in a mechanical voice. "We just blew up four thousand dollars of school property."

You look back at Tina, who, for once, is speechless.

You stand up slowly and put your hands on the back of Jack's chair. An impulse to take care of him comes over you. You rub his shoulders. "We're all in this together, Jack."

Jack tilts his head and regards you with his lips pressed together. "That's one thousand dollars per Digital Detective. You sure about this?"

You look at Tina, who hesitates. You nod slowly, and then she does.

Suddenly, Jack shoots to his feet. "Mr. Purdue," he says, tapping his headset.

The four of you move quickly. Jack packs his stuff into his briefcase while you grab a loose piece of printer paper and scribble, "out of order." You find some tape and slap the note on the demolished computer. You're out the back door, just as you hear the front one opening.

Jack is silent as he walks toward the front door to untape his remote microphone.

"I'll see you later," Tina says. "That assembly for the high tech fair is today. The president of Cye-Tek will be there."

"I guess," Jack says listlessly.

You can feel another presence watching. The three of you turn at the same time to see Jason, a few feet away. He fixes you with a baleful look, one eye blurred by the scratched lens, fit crookedly back into his glasses frame.

"The virus," he says. "Now the school has it, too."

"There's no cure?" Jack asks.

Jason shakes his head glumly. "No cure."

6
GOOD VS. EVIL

The assembly is in the school auditorium after last period. It's optional, but a lot of kids have come because they want to see Sandra Cye, president of Cye-Tek, maker of INSECT INVADERS. The event is open to adults as well, so you wind your way through a mix of kids, teachers, and parents as you search for Satellite Jack and the others.

Jack has planted himself in the second row. He's fiddling with the frame of his headset. You realize he's added a small digital video camera to the contraption.

Randy joins you, and then Tina. You all watch Jack work for a minute. "Going to broadcast the event?" you ask.

Jack's been known to wear the headset to class or to lunch and beam the images to his computer at home, where they go up on his web site. But today he shakes his head. "This is for the investigation."

"How are you doing?" Randy asks him with concern. "I heard about the melt..."

"Shh!" Jack hisses. His attention stays fixed on the camera as he tightens it to the frame. "We don't need to blab it all over the school. All I know is, we're going to nail whoever did it. It was no accident. They're going to pay."

Randy raises his eyebrows. "What do you mean?"

"I mean that virus was planted. It was on the game disk."

All three of you stare at him. Jack checks the apparatus one more time, then places it on his head. Immediately, titters come from the row behind you.

"Mission control to Satellite Jack," a boy barks through cupped hands. "It's time for you to return to whatever alien planet you came from." Two girls, sitting with him, giggle.

When Jack ignores him, the boy reaches out and flicks Jack's headset with his finger. Tina whirls in her seat and bores a hole into him with her eyes. At first, he just makes a face, which sets the girls giggling again. Tina's gaze doesn't waver, though, and she contracts her mouth ever so slightly, like now she's about to really get mad. The laughter stops. It amazes you how Tina can do that.

Jack pretends nothing happened. He gestures for you, Randy, and Tina to lean in closer. "I thought about how the virus emerged," he says in a low voice. "It couldn't have been from some external source. It was fully integrated with the game."

"But who...why?" you sputter.

"Good question. Somebody who wants to sabotage the game, obviously."

"Wait a minute," Tina says. "We were using the bootleg disk, which we found down at the dock. Do you think the virus is just on the pirate version, or is it in all of them?"

"I don't know," Jack admits. "We've got some research to do."

The sound of someone blowing into a microphone makes you look up to the stage. It's Kyle Purdue, the computer lab teacher. He has wedged himself into a student desk to one side of the stage. In the center, seated behind folding tables, are the three guests, each with a mike at their table.

"We're ready to start...if we could have quiet please..." Kyle waits for the audience to settle down. As always, he's wearing his dark blue work shirt and running shoes. A strand of black hair curls over his forehead.

"Welcome to the opening day of our High Tech Career Fair," Kyle begins. "It's the first time we've done this, and I think you'll find it very informative. The fair will continue through the weekend. Some of the companies we've invited will have booths set up in the gym, so you can talk to them one on one. You'll learn more about what they do—and what *you* can do in the exciting future of high tech.

"This afternoon, we kick off the fair with a very special panel discussion among three leaders of the industry, who are very kindly giving up some of their valuable time to talk to us today. To your left, we have Russ Hodges, project engineer at DriveStar, a company that makes disk drives."

A man wearing a business suit with large wire-rim glasses and a pointy chin folds his hands and nods. A few people clap politely.

"In the middle," Kyle continues, "is Darren Cox, founder of Zeus Protection Systems. His company is right here in Crescent Bay. Darren designs software that fixes computer bugs, viruses, and other problems, which we encounter in the cyber age."

Darren Cox gets some applause, and responds with a fit of coughing and a mock salute. He sports a mustache and shaggy sandy-blond hair that shows just enough ear to reveal a ring in his earlobe. He looks to be in his late thirties. You can see under the table that he's wearing khaki shorts.

"And to your right, Sandra Cye, CEO of Cye-Tek, whose division, TerrorStruck Games, produced a computer game called INSECT INVADERS."

Applause resounds through the auditorium. Sandra appears to be in her twenties, with blond hair clipped sportily short. She's wearing a cream-colored silk shirt and black pants. The clapping won't stop, so she stands up and raises her hands for quiet. This only brings more applause, along with some whoops. Sandra smiles, reaches down into a bag by her chair, and lifts out an action figure from the game. It's a two-foot tall Praying Mantis. But instead of praying, it's crushing a three-inch human between its forelegs. The audience goes wild.

She raises a fist and shouts, "Mega Mantis rules!"

Kyle frowns and tries to get the noise under control. "All right, that's enough. We'll begin with Mr. Hodges. Suppose you tell us all about disk drives."

Russ Hodges rambles for a while about drives driving the computer industry in previous decades. "No matter what memory storage medium we use in the future," he says, "there will be a wealth of career opportunities in the field of high tech."

Tina and Jack both fake snores and pretend to fall asleep. "Cut it out," you whisper, trying not to laugh.

It's Darren Cox's turn next. He regards the audience silently for a few moments, slowly shaking his head. Then he grins. "Boy, I wish I was your age. There is so much *cool* stuff coming—and you're the ones who are going to get to design and play with it all. I envy you."

He goes on to talk about how companies are always rushing products to market too fast and how Zeus has to come in and design ways to fix the problems which arise. "It's amazing how much money you can make cleaning up other people's messes," he concludes.

Now, comes the moment everyone has been waiting for. The cheers begin the moment Kyle announces Sandra's first name. When they finally die down, she leans close to speak into her microphone. She has a warm, throaty voice.

"I suppose you're all wondering how we came up with the idea for INSECT INVADERS. Well, let me tell you a little story about my first house in Silicon Valley and its termites."

Suddenly, a voice cries out from the back of the auditorium. "That's not how it started! Tell the truth! You stole it from me!"

You twist in your seat. It's Bug Man. He's standing on a chair and shaking his fist at the stage. While kids back away, you see school officials rushing toward him.

"Get him out of here," Kyle mutters into his microphone.

"The avengers are already here," Bug Man declares. "Your heart shall be weighed against a feather, Sandra Cye..."

Sandra gives him an indulgent smile, as he's being hustled to the exit. "Thank you for sharing, Arthur." She pauses and explains, "He's been trying to make me give him a job for years. You'd think no one had ever seen an insect before him."

Sandra brushes some imaginary lint from her sleeve and continues with her story. But Bug Man's interruption is only the first. From the corner of your eye, you now see a figure rise in the third row. It's Jason the Destroyer.

"I don't care about termites!" he shouts. "What about the

virus? Your game has a virus that..."

"Jason," Kyle breaks in, "you can ask questions later."

But Jason doesn't stop. He's shaking with anger. "I was the best player around, and your game destroyed my computer!"

To your surprise, Sandra Cye doesn't brush him off. Instead, she gets up and crouches at the edge of the platform. She wears a sympathetic look on her face.

"Jason—is that your name? Jason, I'm really sorry to hear about that. I've scorched a few hard drives myself, and I know how bad it feels. I'll personally see to it that your computer is replaced, courtesy of Cye-Tek. All right?"

Jason gapes at her in awe. He nods slowly and sits down.

You nudge Jack. "Maybe she'll replace..."

"Forget it," he snaps. "I'm not admitting I fried a hard drive in front of all these people."

"All right," Kyle says with impatience. "Let's get back to our program."

But Sandra Cye has barely seated herself again when an adult voice rings out, "INSECT INVADERS *is* a virus. It should be banned!"

"Must be SICK," you whisper to Jack.

"Cye-Tek out of our children's brains!" another voice chimes in.

Sandra is unfazed. She just shakes her head with amusement as the two protesters are shown the exit. Once some order is restored, she says, "You can count on it. If we invent something new and innovative that kids think is fun, some adult out there will try to ruin it. Probably, the same thing happened when the telephone was invented. Some parent said, 'Oh no, now my teenager's going to spend all night talking to her friends.'"

This draws laughter from the audience. But Kyle Purdue squirms to draw himself upright in his chair. You're surprised at what he has to say.

"That may be true, but isn't there a point worth discussing here? Yes, there's always resistance to new technology. But doesn't it come down to how we use the technology? It can be used for good, but it can be used for bad, too."

Suddenly Kyle stops. His eyes narrow, as he spots something, which he obviously doesn't like, in the back of the auditorium.

You turn to look. There in the aisle, leaning against the wall, is a teenager with hair that's short in front and long in the back. He's wearing a flannel shirt that looks awfully familiar.

You swivel back quickly, putting two and two together. "It's him!" you whisper. "The guy who chased us!"

"Yeah, he's got the hockey hair that Walter described. Don't worry," Randy whispers back to you. "We'll take care of him together."

You sit frozen in your chair. Meanwhile, Kyle picks up the thread of his thought. "I'm just wondering, Ms. Cye—in this game, all you do is go around crushing insects. You don't learn anything about them. In fact, what information there is, is inaccurate. Is this really the best use of our technology?"

Sandra looks miffed by the question. "Mr. Purdue, you know very well this game is not meant to be an educational product. It's purely for fun. Even so, I think you can find a number of positives..."

"Wait a minute, wait a minute," Darren Cox breaks in, spreading his arms to take charge. "Aren't we missing the real point here? You can debate until you're blue in the face whether a product is good for kids or bad for kids. Who really knows? I think the real question is this: is a product well-made or poorly-made? Was it shipped to market too quickly in order to make a fast buck, or did the publisher take the time to make a product with integrity?"

"What's your point, Darren?" Sandra shoots back. "Think you can make a better game than INSECT INVADERS? We both know you can't."

Darren's face reddens. "Admit it, Sandra. You've been holding out on us. Even when this young man, Jason, here in front, told the world that his computer had been destroyed, you wouldn't come clean. INSECT INVADERS has a virus!"

The effect of his words on the crowd is incredible. Pandemonium breaks out. There are groans and screams. Everyone starts talking at once.

"Where's the bug? Where's the bug?"

"Can we get our money back?"

"What about the secret level?"

Sandra hunches over her microphone and tries desperately to explain that there have been only a few reports of problems.

But Darren's voice overrides hers. "The good news...THE GOOD NEWS, EVERYBODY...is that Zeus is right this moment ready to release a fix for the virus. Your computers are safe!"

It's hard to know if anyone is listening. Kids are milling around, asking each other if their computers have blown up.

Kyle is dashing across the stage, trying to quiet everyone down. Sandra is running her hands through her hair, repeating Cye-Tek's URL over and over, saying there's information posted on their web site. Russ Hodges is playing with Mega Mantis. Darren Cox sits back, heaves his feet up on the table, and appears to be enjoying it all.

You snap a couple of pictures of the uproar. You don't know if they'll help your investigation, but they'll make good images when Randy writes about the event on his web site.

That turns out to be the last thing on Randy's mind. He grabs your arm, blurring your last picture. Jerking his thumb toward the back of the auditorium, he says, "That guy, he's getting away. Let's go after him!"

You have no time to object. Randy drags you to the aisle, and Tina pushes from behind. You fight your way toward the exit. A glimpse of the haircut tells you that the teenager is ducking out the right hand door.

Now you're leading the charge. "This way!" you say, turning right. You race down the hallway, dodging kids and parents alike. But you're not gaining any ground.

Randy jumps up and sees a soccer teammate ahead. "Cooper!" he calls out. "Stop the hockey hair!"

A moment later, you catch sight of Cooper staggering backward into a wall. "Which way did he go?" Randy asks him.

Cooper just shakes his head, two fingers touching his bloody lip. "I don't know. Dude, why'd you ask me to..."

But Randy doesn't stay to answer. He charges ahead, and you're on his heels.

You reach the end of the hallway. It branches to the left and right. "You guys, go down there," Randy instructs Tina and Jack, pointing to the right. "We'll go this way."

You and Randy move quickly down the hall, looking in every classroom, testing every door. There's no sign of the guy. At the end of the hall, there is an exit. You push through it.

You find yourself on a landing at the top of a concrete stairway, overlooking the school parking lot. You grab Randy's arm and point to a car in the middle of the lot.

"The blue pickup!" Randy says. "Do you think it's his?"

"Maybe," you say, leading the way down the stairs. Pumped from the pursuit, you forget about caution. All you can think about is the chance to gather evidence on the truck.

You've already pulled your scanner out of your pack when you get there. You take a scan of the tire treads.

Randy has discovered that the front door of the truck is open. He slips inside and roots through the glove compartment. You get in the front seat and dust the steering wheel for fingerprints.

"This guy is Travis, all right," Randy says, reading the truck's registration. "Just like you thought."

Suddenly, his satisfaction turns to alarm. You follow his eyes. Bobbing above the roofs of the parked cars is the haircut. No doubt about it, he's coming your way. There's also no doubt that he'll see you if you bolt out of the truck.

"Come on!" Randy says. He's already shut the glove compartment and has squeezed halfway through a sliding window that separates the camper shell in the back of the truck from the cab in front.

"But..."

"No choice!"

You toss your pack through the sliding window, then dive through it. Randy pulls you into the back, where you collapse onto one another. Quickly he reaches up to slide the window most of the way closed.

A second later, the truck door opens. Travis jumps into the driver's seat and slams the door shut.

"What the...?" he curses when he finds the dust on the steering wheel. But he's in a hurry. He fires up the engine and lays tracks out of the parking lot, sending you and Randy crashing into the side of the flatbed in back.

7
THE INFESTATION

The midnight blue pickup truck lurches down the street. Travis is not exactly the greatest driver. He slams on the brakes every time he stops. He mashes the accelerator when he starts again, turning you and Randy into human pinballs in the back.

The truck makes a sudden stop in the middle of a block. The horn blares. A moment later, you hear heels on the pavement. Someone gets in on the passenger side.

"Hey," Travis says. You hear some kind of rustling in front, then the truck lurches into traffic again. After a minute of silence, Travis complains, "Aw geez, do you have to do that in here?"

Randy takes a quick peek up front. "She's plucking her eyebrows," he whispers.

Your eyes meet and, in spite of everything, you have to clap your hand over your mouth, to keep from laughing.

"Clean up after yourself, okay?" Travis adds.

"Right, like you're going to notice a couple little hairs in here," a female voice answers.

You'd recognize the voice anywhere. It's Tammy. As her perfume begins to penetrate the back of the truck, you get a sick feeling in your stomach.

Another minute goes by. "Hey Tammy, what kind of junk

is this that you've got all over my steering wheel? It looks like something out of your makeup bag."

"That's not my junk. That's your junk."

"Well, I don't like it. It's getting all over my fingers."

"Well, clean up your truck for a change."

"I keep it clean. You know that."

You have to agree with Travis. Except for a couple of empty cardboard boxes and some heavy chains that rattle with each turn, the back of the truck is nice and tidy.

"Where are we going anyway?" Tammy complains. "I thought you were taking me out."

"Yeah, well, I've got to stop by the warehouse for a minute. Gotta resupply. The game's selling like hotcakes."

You grab Randy's arm. It seems you've got your man.

Or is it the other way around? It's more like he's got you. When he picks up the new boxes, he'll surely load them into the back, where you are.

Randy slides beside you and whispers into your ear. "If he catches us, you run for it. I'll deal with Travis."

"But..."

He silences you with a squeeze of your neck. "Your job is to get the cops."

After a few more turns, the truck lurches to a final stop. Travis kills the engine. "I'll be right back," he says.

"Is there a rest room in there?" Tammy asks.

Please say yes, you think.

"Oh man, didn't you already do all your makeup at home?"

Tammy lets out a sigh. "Fine. I'll do it right here."

Your heart sinks. How are you going to escape with Tammy on guard?

A minute passes. You try to keep down your rising panic. When Randy taps you on the shoulder, you jump.

"Ready?" he whispers.

"What?"

But he's already scooted up to the window. He takes a breath. Then in one motion he slides it open, pokes his head through, and says, "Hi!"

Tammy shrieks and drops her makeup kit. She's out the door in a flash, running into the warehouse, screaming, "Travis! Travis!"

Randy squeezes out of the back, through the window. You scramble after him, tumbling into the front seat and out Tammy's open door.

The truck is parked to the right of the warehouse entrance. There's a narrow passage between the cinder block side wall of the warehouse and the razor wire fence of the next lot over. The two of you dash down the passage toward the back of the warehouse. You figure there's less chance of Travis seeing you there, than if you just take off down the street.

As you get to the corner, you take a quick glance back. Travis is peering inside the truck, but he doesn't look your way. You turn the corner, head down the next block, and then zigzag your way through the North End until it seems safe to slow down.

"Good work," Randy says, holding out his hand for a slap.

"I don't think we're home free yet," you warn him. "We need a hiding place." The sound of squealing tires, a few blocks away, confirms your fear.

You're at the waterfront now, with its cranes, hoists, and docks. You spy a handmade sign that says FRESH FISH.

Following the arrow through a puddle-filled boatyard, you find an aluminum shed with its big rollup gate open.

An old Vietnamese man greets you inside. He's standing over a chopping block with a heavy cleaver. His apron is streaked with fish guts. "Hello, what'd you like?"

"We're just looking," you say.

He smiles. "Fine."

You linger in the fish market, among the oysters, mussels, and bright orange salmon, all laid out in metal bins, filled with crushed ice. One bin is filled with water, and inside, crabs crawl lazily over one another.

"Do you have the MicroJack?" Randy asks. "Let's check in with the others."

You power up the device and send a message saying that after a close encounter with Travis, you've found the ware-house. Oh, and by the way, you're safe.

"Good," Tina messages back. "Let's investigate."

"Now?" you wonder.

Randy places a finger on his chin. "Yeah, maybe this is the perfect time. It's the last place Travis will look for us. Besides, he's got Tammy with him. She just wants to go on their date."

You send the message. Jack quickly replies, "No way."

But Tina has other ideas. "Let's do it. Satellite Jack can stay at mission control."

Jack agrees reluctantly. You send Tina the address of the fish market. She says that she'll be right down.

While you wait for her, Randy buys a couple of oysters. You give him a sidelong glance. "You like oysters?"

He shrugs. "We've been here for half an hour. I figure that we should buy something."

*   *   *

You, Tina, and Randy approach the cinder block warehouse warily. All seems quiet. Finally, you stand in front of it, a low gray building with a few windows cut into the sides. A loading dock is in the center of the front wall, its gate closed and locked. On the right hand side is a short flight of stairs and a brown door.

"Now what?" you ask.

Randy checks up and down the street. "Let's investigate."

Tina points at the brown door. "The first question is, how do we get in?"

Continue your investigation on the Digital Detective web site:

http://www.ddmysteries.com

and enter the key phrase **WAREHOUSE**

When you're done investigating, the web site will tell you where to keep reading in the book.

The three of you all stare at each other, and you begin to have regrets. The street outside is quiet. Maybe you didn't need to be in such a hurry to leave.

"Do you think we found some good stuff?" you ask Randy and Tina.

Tina shrugs. "Yeah, some...there were a few more places I would have liked to look."

"Me, too," Randy admits.

You stop in your tracks. "Maybe we left too early. Maybe there's more to find here. What do you guys think?

Randy nods. "I'm willing to keep looking."

"Let's do it," Tina agrees.

Return to your investigation of the warehouse on the Digital Detectives web site:

http://www.ddmysteries.com

and enter the key phrase **OUTSIDE**

When you're done investigating, the web site will tell you where to keep reading in the book.

You open your eyes to find yourself slumped on the concrete floor of the warehouse, your ears being assaulted by heavy metal music.

You're wedged between Randy and Tina, your hands tied to the metal shelving on which the bootleg games are stacked. As you shake the grogginess out of your head, you realize that the music is blasting from the computer on the desk, where Travis is sitting with his feet up.

"Could you turn that down please?" you say.

Travis swivels in the chair. He strokes the fur of the cat who lies purring in his lap. But the one with the smile of feline satisfaction is Travis. His mouth moves. You can't hear him over the thundering power chords.

"What?" You try to jerk your arms free. They're well tied, but your motion awakens Tina and Randy.

The music stops abruptly. Travis smiles again and says, "I guess I'm the cat who got the canary, aren't I?"

"What are you gonna do now, Travis?" Randy demands. "Go ahead and beat us up. I dare you. You'll spend a lot more time in juvenile detention for that, than for making pirated games."

Travis just snorts. "Oh, you don't have to worry about *me*. I'm not the one who's going to decide what to do with you."

"Who is?" you ask.

Travis doesn't answer. Instead, he tosses the cat off his lap, gets up, and bends over you. You can see the blackheads on his nose and smell hamburger on his breath. "You think you're pretty smart, don't you?"

His eyes drill into yours. You have to look away. Then all

of a sudden you start writhing. Something is crawling on your neck. A beetle.

Travis seems amused by your little jig. The bug crawls over your jaw and begins circling toward your ear. Travis reaches out and flicks it off, giving your earlobe a good snap in the process.

He goes back to the desk, clears a space, and sits on it. His cowboy boots slide the chair back and forth, as he thinks about what he's going to say next.

"I don't know what you're talking about with these games. You've got nothing on me. All I do is feed the cat and clean the warehouse."

"Wrong," Tina states. "We've got your fingerprints from the dock. And your tire tracks."

"Old Walter can identify you," you add. "You sold him games."

Travis eyes your backpack, which contains your investigation tools, sitting on the floor.

"All the evidence is safe with our friend Jack," Tina says. "So don't think you can destroy it."

Travis kicks the chair toward you, stands up, and begins to pace. "You little twerps."

Abruptly he stops and throws his arms into the air. "What do you care anyway? All I'm doing is giving kids what they want at a decent price. They love this stupid game. Cye-Tek charges an arm and a leg—*that's* the crime."

You nod, hoping he'll go on.

"So what's the beef?" he continues. "Cye-Tek is ripping them off. What's so bad about saving kids some money?"

"It's illegal," Randy points out.

"Plus, the virus," you say.

"What virus?" he demands.

"The spider virus, in the secret level," you tell him. "We know all about it."

"*You* may know all about it, but I don't," Travis says. "I've never played the game in my life."

You glance at Randy, then Tina. You can tell they think the same thing you do: Travis's ignorance seems real.

"The game, at least the bootleg version, is spreading a deadly virus to kids' computers," you explain. "It fries hard drives like eggs in hot grease."

"It happened to us this morning," Tina adds. "And you should've seen Jason's face, after his computer died."

Travis's fists are clenched, his jaw tight. "Wait a minute. You're telling me this game—" he slams a fist against one of the boxes on the shelf—"is blowing up kids' computers?"

You nod. "Yeah. Deliberately blowing up kids' computers."

"Man, nobody told me that was in the plan."

"Nobody who?" Randy asks quickly.

"I don't know who runs this scam," Travis says with a wave of his hand. "I just know...well, never mind."

"Skeet?" you ask.

"Yeah. But he's not the brains, believe me, just the muscle."

"What about Annie? Is she the master mind?"

"Maybe. I never heard of her until the other night, when Skeet said something." Travis runs his hand over his head and tugs at the long locks in back. He can see your skeptical expression. "Look, I'm being totally straight with you here. I don't ask. They just pay me and I perform a service."

"They pay you pretty well, too," Randy notes, picking up

on one of the clues you just found. "We looked at that account book. Lots of money paid out to you, but none coming in from you. Why's that?"

Travis's face softens as he thinks. "I know, it's kinda weird. Usually, not only do I have to buy the product, I have to give a cut back to the...manufacturer. This outfit, they *paid* me to sell it *and* said I could keep the profits. Just as long as I sold the game for below a certain price."

"Whew." You whistle. "It sounds like they just want to get the game out there."

"But if they're not in it for the money...then why?" Randy wonders.

"Maybe..."A horrible realization comes over you. "Maybe, it's just to spread the virus. That's all they care about."

"That's pretty freaky," Travis remarks.

The rest of you fall silent in agreement.

"Have you ever taken a computer class?" Tina asks suddenly.

You wonder what put that thought into Tina's head.

So does Travis. He puts his hands on his hips. "No, I've never taken no *stupid* computer class. What's it to you, anyway?"

Tina just nods and gives him a smile.

"Look," Randy jumps in. "We can see that you're as mad about what this game is doing to kids as we are. So whaddya say we call a truce? You let us go. We won't turn you in. We'll try to catch whoever's spreading this virus."

"If you do, I'll give evidence against the slimeball, too," Travis fumes. "I got nothing against these kids. They're my *customers*."

"Good," Randy agrees.

Travis stands with his hands in his pockets for a moment, gazing sidelong at the three of you. Finally, he unsheathes a knife from his belt. You tense as he approaches.

"You sure you're not calling the cops on me?" he demands.

"Promise," Randy answers.

He shakes the knife at you. "Because if you do..."

Then he takes the knife and cuts each of you loose.

8
PREYING MANTIS

"My brain hurts," Jack says

When Satellite Jack admits his brain hurts, you know you're up against some heavy duty mental lifting. The Digital Detectives are gathered at the picnic table in the park. It's Saturday morning, and you're trying to untangle all of the new information that you've collected in the past 24 hours.

"We have to take a logical approach," Tina declares. "Do it like the police do it. First, we make a list of suspects and a list of witnesses. Then, we figure out who belongs on which list."

She takes out a piece of paper, draws a line down the middle, and starts writing names.

SUSPECTS	WITNESSES
Skeet	
Travis	
other pirates	
Annie	
Jason	
Old Walter	
Bug Man	
S.I.C.K.	
Mr. Purdue	
Sandra Cye	
Darren Cox	
Russ Hodges	

"Whoa!" Randy exclaims. "Everybody's a suspect!"

"Sure," Tina responds. "Until we come up with a good reason to move them to the Witness side."

"So, how do we decide that?" you ask.

"Okay," Tina explains, "how my dad says it works is that you ask three questions about a suspect. One, do they have a motive for committing the crime? Two, do they have the means to commit the crime? Three, did they have the opportunity to commit the crime?"

"Motive, means, opportunity," you repeat. "But... are we sure what the crime is yet?"

"It's pretty clear to me now," Jack answers. "There's computer game piracy, sure. But that's nano compared to the perpetrator's real goal. Which is nothing less than to sabotage INSECT INVADERS, and/or Cye-Tek, and/or maybe the whole computer game industry. Even if they have to torch thousands of kids' computers to do it."

No one speaks for a minute. The awesome scope of this evil plan boggles the mind. Judging from the silence of your friends, their minds are boggled, too. Finally Randy shakes his head. "Why? What could make someone do that?"

"That's what we have to figure out," Tina declares.

"Okay," you say. "So *motive* means you have some reason to sabotage the game—a *major* reason, otherwise you wouldn't take the risk. *Means* means that you've got the tools and skills to plant the virus. So, it's got be someone who knows computer programming, right?"

"An ace coder," Jack agrees.

"*Opportunity* means you have a way to get your hands on the game, make the bootlegs, and sell them, with the help of guys like Travis."

"Our best suspect is Annie," Tina decides. "The only problem is, we don't know a single thing about her. The only hard evidence we have is that shipping log."

"Okay then, let's go back to the three questions you said to ask, Tina," Randy suggests. "Start with motive. Who's got the strongest motive? I'd say it's those SICK people."

"Yeah, but they're fossilized. They don't know a thing about computers. They couldn't design the virus," Jack points out.

"Unless Mr. Purdue is helping them," Tina says. "Didn't it kind of sound like he was on their side at the assembly?"

"He barely even tried to hide it," Randy confirms.

"Kyle knows computers," Jack allows. "But whoever did this is *good*."

"Jack," you say, "didn't you read that file we found in the warehouse? Kyle coded games for Instinct Software in Texas before he became a teacher."

"Wow," Jack says, impressed. "*Means*."

"Then, there's Sandra Cye," Randy muses. "What if she's trying to cover up some big mistake her company made? Did you see how fast she offered to pay for Jason's computer?"

"Or there's Darren Cox," you add. "If he really does have a cure for the virus, he'll make some big money."

"He's got the fix, all right," Jack says. "Exterminator. It's being released Monday. Only problem is, it can't fix computers that are already toast. So, we still owe the school a four thousand dollar system."

This thought sobers everyone for a minute. Then, Tina says, "One person who for sure doesn't know computers is

Travis."

"You're making an assumption," Jack asserts. "What if he was lying?"

"Oh come on, Jack, you weren't there. You've got to just accept our judgment," Tina chides.

This evokes a chorus of responses, some agreeing with Tina and some with Jack. Pretty soon everyone is proclaiming their own theory of who should and shouldn't be on the Suspect list.

Tina waves the sheet of paper in the air. "Okay, be quiet! *I've* got the list. I know Jack's not going to let me keep it. But I say he shouldn't keep it, either, because he never believes anyone."

Jack looks kind of hurt, but what Tina says is true. His opinions are already strong enough. Better that someone else takes charge of the Suspect list.

Randy takes hold of one edge of the sheet. "May I?"

"I guess..." Tina says.

"Not for me." Randy pushes the paper over to you. "Here. You're in charge of the list. You decide when to move someone from the Suspect side to the Witness side. Everyone agree?"

He looks around the table. Jack scowls at Tina, who scowls right back, only harder. She grits her teeth, making fun of his expression. Finally, Jack laughs and goes along with the plan. Tina agrees too.

You look down at the paper. "I'm not going to do anything right now," you announce. "We need to ask more questions first. I think we should split up and interview the suspects. We'll all report what we find, and then make our decisions about the list."

"Good idea," Randy agrees.

Jack raises his hand. "If I may suggest—if her royal highness Tina will allow—I'll also draw up a timeline, so that we can see exactly when everything in the case occurred."

"Good," you say. "So, let's see...which suspects do each of us want to interview?"

*   *   *

How did I get stuck with Bug Man? you ask yourself, as you get on your bike to pedal down to Branch Avenue.

But you know the answer. Since you're the keeper of the list, everyone else got to choose who they wanted to interview first. You got whoever was left.

This is the last thing you expected to find yourself doing when you moved to Crescent Bay this past summer. You're kind of wondering what you've gotten yourself into. It's a big compliment to be put in charge of the list. But it's also pretty daunting to be riding downtown to cross-examine an adult—not to mention scary, when the adult is Bug Man.

You wonder if the others feel nervous as well. Or is it only you? Tina's a bold girl, afraid of nothing, though you worry it might get her into trouble some day. Jack's very sure of his intelligence, but then again, he can get seriously shy in public. You imagine it'll be easiest for Randy, because he's a little older and fairly confident.

It's a funny group, you muse, as you turn onto Branch Avenue. They're all so different. Except for you—you've got a little bit in common with all of them. Like Tina, you're a board rider. Like Jack, you've got some brains. Not as many as Jack, of course, but you can usually keep up with him. As for Randy, you're just happy that someone as cool as Randy even talks to you. But he's let it been known more than once that there's nothing he values more than a true and honest friend. You guess he cares more about that than the adulation he gets for being the top goal-scoring forward on the soccer team.

At first, you wondered what made this group friends before you met. Especially Jack and Tina, who seem so different. Make that Jack and *anybody*. No doubt about it, Jack is an odd guy. A lot of people don't "get" Jack. They think he's weird, nerdy, and arrogant because he's so smart. And the truth is, they're right. He *can* be arrogant. There are a lot of people Jack doesn't "get" either. But you're someone who appreciates his talents. You also kind of like how he's brilliant and timid at the same time, even if he's a pain now and then. The fact that you accept him for who he is makes him appreciate you a whole lot. The same goes for Randy and Tina.

Tina and Jack have known each other since kindergarten. Maybe that's why they're comfortable with one another, you muse. Sure, they make each other mad sometimes, but there's also some mysterious bond there. Then, you remember Tina saying that she never hung out with Jack and Randy as much she does now. So maybe, actually, *you're* the one who's brought this group together.

All of a sudden, you slam on your bicycle brakes. You've been trolling up and down the avenue, in search of Bug Man. Now you spot him going into a cafe. After you've parked your bike, you take a deep breath and open the door. How are you going to start a conversation with a weird guy like him?

You're glad to see other customers in the cafe. Bug Man is sitting at a table with a steaming cup of coffee and a big brownie in front of him. He's outfitted in his usual insect regalia, and is also wearing a rumpled sun hat, even though it's cloudy out.

You order a hot chocolate and carry it to a chair close to the door, one table down from Bug Man.

One of Bug Man's eyes remains fixed on his coffee, but the other one seems to be watching you. You look down quickly and take a sip of your drink. It burns your mouth. You draw in quick breaths, slurping to cool it off.

Bug Man grimaces. "Don't you hate that?"

You nod and make fanning motions in front of your mouth.

"I know you," he adds in a flat voice. His gaze remains fixed on you.

It's now or never, you decide. "You were at Walter's..."

"Not just that." His face is blank as a mask. You wish he'd show some kind of emotion—any emotion, to give you a clue what he's thinking about you.

"Yeah?" you manage to say.

He sips his coffee slowly and deliberately. "You're up to something, you and your friends. I haven't figured out whose side you're on yet."

You decide to take the plunge. "You mean...about the virus?"

"Bah!" He flicks his wrist as if slapping aside a mosquito.

His head sinks lower on his neck, and he regards you through hooded eyes. Then he sits up abruptly, crosses his legs, and presses his hands together, as if in prayer. "The mantis. Do you know what *mantis* means?"

You shake your head.

"It means prophet. Because of the insect's attitude of prayer." He lifts his eyes angel-like to the ceiling. Then his lip curls and his fingers deform into a claw. They swoop down on the brownie, rip off a bit, and take it to his mouth.

"Of course, we both know what it's really about, don't we?" he goes on, chewing. "Prey, not prayer. The mantis uses its forelegs to crush its victims. Just like Cye-Tek."

You nod, encouraging him to keep going.

"But!" He raises a finger. "What happens if one of its victims fights back? It happens, you know. In Mexico, they eat stink bugs. Alive. Sometimes the bugs bite back. On the tongue of the eater."

You involuntarily stick out your own tongue in disgust.

"Precisely. That's just how Sandra Cye feels right now."

You cock your head. "So, you know her?"

Bug Man heaves a deep, sorrowful sigh. Instead of answering, he asks you an unexpected question. "Do you know what happens to you when you die?"

Huh? "Not a clue," you reply.

He thinks carefully. "You see, after you die, your heart will be weighed against a feather. If your heart is lighter than the feather, you go to the good place."

He pauses to finger an amulet resting on his chest. "The Scarab protects your heart from the heart stealer. The heart stealer has the body of a lion and comes with a knife. The

Scarab, prophet of rebirth, drives him away."

"Uh huh," you say.

"So, you see."

"Can you explain it a little more?"

"The beetle is our protector. The heart stealer is bad enough: he preys upon our doubt. But there's one who's worse: a protector who goes bad. You may be able to misuse the power of the protector for a little while, but in the long run it cannot be corrupted. He who tries to do so will suffer terribly—terribly!"

You wonder what all of this has to do with the game. "Is there a beetle scene in INSECT INVADERS?"

Bug Man's eyes grow wide. "*Is there a beetle scene?* Holy rolypoly, it's awesome. You chase all these beetles through these dung tunnels, and they're rolling big balls of it at you, and splat! splat! splat!"

His arms are waving around now and he's got a big smile on his face.

"Okay," you say slowly, "I'll check it out."

You gulp down the last of your drink. Bug Man sips his coffee. Then he scoots forward, holding out his hand. "I'm Arthur, by the way. You probably know me by another name."

You shake his hand. Something sticks to your palm.

"Oops, sorry!" Arthur says, licking the brownie frosting from his fingers. He laughs. He's calm now, at ease. It occurs to you that he can be a perfectly normal person when he feels like it.

You wonder if you should ask him more questions. His cryptic words and images swirl in your head, making it hard to think. You find yourself standing up and saying, "Well, thanks a lot, Arthur. I'll see you later."

He smiles and gives a good-bye wave. "The infestation has just begun," he says cheerfully. "And remember: the bugs always win."

9
REPORTS FROM THE FIELD

A big yawn that you cannot contain overpowers you after dinner. You can see the look coming from your mom, and quickly cover your mouth.

"Tired?" she asks. "It seems like you've been out a lot lately. Maybe you should go to bed early tonight."

Actually, the idea sounds pretty good. There's nothing you'd rather do than vege out on the living room sofa for a couple of hours and then hit the sack. But you can't. You've got a crime to investigate, reports to read, and suspects to consider. Of course, you don't tell your parents that. At least, not yet.

"Yeah," you agree. "First I need to do a little homework."

"It's a Saturday night," she points out. "Do they really give you that much work?"

"Well, it's a special project that I'm doing with Jack and Tina."

"Really?" you dad says. "What's it about?"

"Um, video games. You know, whether they're good or bad for kids." You think back to what Mr. Purdue said at the panel discussion. "And if they're the best use of our technology."

Your dad nods with approval. "I imagine it depends on the game, doesn't it?"

"That's pretty much what we're saying," you respond, trying to head off any more questions. But then you think of a question of your own. "Do you know anything about computer viruses, Dad? The people who write them?"

"It's not my expertise, but..."

"They're usually loners," your mom says. "They feel like they've been wronged for some reason. Or that no one understands what geniuses they are. So they hack a brilliant bit of code that will get everyone's attention. The curse of it is that if they let the world know who did it, they'll go to jail."

"For how long?" you ask.

Your mom looks at your dad. "The last one I heard about got...what, six years? It depends on how much damage the virus does."

Your dad nods. "Of course, some hackers are just plain malicious. Those are the worst. They're not trying to prove a point, just destroy for the pleasure of it. Kind of like certain video games, come to think of it."

You sag inwardly at the thought. First, because it's baffling and scary that people like that exist in the world—just plain malicious." It sends an unpleasant chill down your spine. Second, because if someone like that made the INSECT INVADERS virus, then there will be no motive for you to track down.

"On the other hand," you mom muses, "maybe, computer games are a good outlet. Maybe, they divert people from doing damage in the real world."

"What's the latest one that's so big?" your dad asks. "BUG RAIDERS?"

86

"INSECT INVADERS," you correct.

"Have you played it?"

You know the question isn't meant as some sort of test. Your parents are pretty good about letting you decide how to spend your spare time. They keep an eye on it, but they also trust you to make good decisions.

"Once or twice," you answer. "You, uh, have to eat all these insects before they eat you."

Your dad grins. "Sounds like fun."

Your mom shoots him a look, then starts clearing the table. You help her do the dishes, then make yourself go to your room and sit down at the computer.

* * *

Reports from the other three Digital Detectives are waiting in your e-mail inbox. You've already written up your talk with Arthur—Bug Man. That part took the longest. The rest will be shorter. The other two suspects you had to contact were Darren Cox and the mysterious Annie.

You set to work finishing your own report. When you're done, you send it out to the others. Then, you download their files and settle in to read them.

YOUR REPORT

If anyone can figure out what Bug Man was talking about, be sure to let me know.

Anyway, after I saw him I rode my bike to Zeus Protection Systems, Darren Cox's company. It's in this little square building in a business park near the airport. It turns out that

I rode all the way down there for nothing. When I went inside, this woman told me that he was at a high-tech fair, at a local school. Duh! I could have just interviewed him there.

Anyway, I talked to her for a few minutes. Her name was Cindy. She was pretty, with curly blond hair, blue eyes, and very smooth skin.

She said it was really nice of him to keep his commitment to the fair, especially since that horrible Sandra Cye was going to be there. "Not only that," she said, "but Darren went to all kinds of extra trouble to get an early shipment of Exterminator for the kids at the fair. Our phone's been ringing off the hook, since he announced it yesterday."

"Why is Sandra Cye so horrible?" I said.

She looked at me like I'd just asked the dumbest question. "She's just mean," she said, "and she made that terrible game. *Why* she's that way, I don't know."

Cindy went back to what she was doing, which was decorating the walls for a party. They're getting ready to celebrate the release of Exterminator on Monday.

I said it was coming out just in time because the virus sounded really nasty. She agreed. She said that Darren thought up the cure for the virus, practically the day it was discovered, and they'd been working on it really hard for over a month.

I asked her if she liked working there. She got all gushy about what a great company it was. It did look like a nice place to hang out—there were beanbag chairs and funny toys to play with everywhere. People were relaxed. Cindy went on and on about Darren. She seemed to think he was some kind of genius. I think that, maybe, she has a crush on him.

I went to school to look for Darren Cox, but the fair had already closed for the day. Then, I came home and tried to find out something about Annie. I looked in the phone book but of course there are lots of Annie's. I did a search on the Web and I found: Annie Oakley, Annie Hall, Orphan Annie, Dirt Bike Annie, Annie's Pickles... In other words, ZERO.

RANDY'S REPORT

Travis: Here's the news—somebody took a tire iron to the headlights on Travis's truck. Boy is he furious. I don't think there's anything he cares about more than that truck.

He got a phone call last night. He couldn't tell who it was because they used a digital modulator to disguise their voice. They said that he better keep selling INSECT INVADERS. Travis figures it couldn't have been Skeet because Skeet doesn't have that kind of technology. Plus, Skeet was out of town (that's why Travis came back to the warehouse to feed the cat).

Anyway, Travis is hopping mad. He wants to get whoever smashed up his truck. We both figure that it must be whoever is behind the INSECT INVADERS plot.

Skeet: I asked around about him down at the harbor. A few people knew him. They said he mostly keeps to himself. He goes to the local bar for a beer and sits at the end and grumbles about how the fish have gotten all fished out of the bay and you can't make a living at it any more.

No one knows what he was up to, but he was seen steaming out of the harbor on his fishing boat the other night.

Someone said that he got back just before dawn this morning.

Pirate gang: I found the other pirates on the south side. It wasn't too hard. Kids down there know where to find them. They mostly just kind of snarled at me once I told them that I wasn't there to buy a game from them. What got them talking was when I told them about Travis's truck. They looked honestly surprised to hear about it. But they loved it, wanted to hear all the details. Anyway, I finally got them to talk about the night at Dock 18. They heard a shipment was coming in on some kind of boat. All they were trying to do was intimidate their rivals. Maybe it worked, because Travis told them he'd wholesale them some bootlegs to sell. But he wanted too much money for them and they told him to get lost.

So I don't know, it doesn't really seem like they're involved. They aren't even selling INSECT INVADERS. There might be a hacker among them who could write the virus, but then, why would they have their enemy, Travis, be the one to spread it?

TINA'S REPORT

Jason the Destroyer: In my humble opinion, Jason is a victim, not a suspect. I go over to his house and he's just moping around. Must be going through some kind of withdrawal, I think. I say we should have a funeral or something for his deceased computer. He takes me seriously. He wants to go dig a hole in the woods right away. But I say we better wait just in case the computer is needed for evidence.

So then I go, "What were you doing down at Dock 18 on

Wednesday night?"

His eyes get all teary. He finally admits that he went down there to buy a copy of the bootleg version of the game, because that was the one with the secret level. Then he gets very dramatic and bursts out, "How I rue the day!"

I'm like, right, maybe you should have thought of that in the first place, Shakespeare. Except what I say is, "My general policy is to stay away from illegal merchandise."

That makes him start bawling right in front of me. So, that's why I think he's innocent.

Sandra Cye: I try to talk to her at the fair in the gym. There's eight million kids swarming around her table, of course. Maybe if I had some bug spray I could have had more time to chat.

Anyway, I fight through the crowd to finally get to her. She's lapping up all the attention. She doesn't like it much when, instead of telling her how great the game is, I ask about the virus.

"I've already discussed that question," she says. "We believe that the virus is only on the pirated copies." She raises her voice. "Don't buy bootlegs, people!"

"Yeah, but what if it's not just the bootleg?" I say.

"Look, it's not a major problem," she snaps.

Some dumbo hits me on the shoulder and goes, "Yeah, that's yesterday's news. Go buy the Exterminator."

I give him a serious look and suddenly he's got somewhere else to be.

"You must be glad that Darren Cox has a cure for it," I say to Sandra.

If ice can get any colder, she does. "Call our Customer Service line, if you need help."

These other kids start yelling for her to sign autographs, so I figure I've got one more question left. I ask her what kind of car she drives, as if I really care.

She tosses her head and says it's a Lexus. Like, *naturally*.

So, I go outside to the parking lot and there's only one Lexus there and I get a scan of the tires.

Now, I'm just doing a job, so I don't take the whole thing with her personally. But if you ask me, this woman is capable of anything.

Russ Hodges: Right. Mr. Big. I still say this guy is such a good citizen—he comes to a full and complete stop at every sign.

But, I'm doing my job, so I talk to him at the fair. Nobody is at his table, of course. But actually, he's really nice to me. He played INSECT INVADERS before the fair started this morning and he's all charged up about the wasps in the brain-eating scene.

We watch the Zeus table for a while, which has almost as many kids crowded around it as the Cye-Tek table. Exterminator is selling like hotcakes. I ask if it makes him feel bad that no one's coming to his table. He just smiles and says, "No, I understand it. I was the same way at your age. You've just got to do what you're good at, and disk drives happen to be my strength. I'd never make it in the game industry."

Anyway, he gave me a coupon for 15% off a new disk drive, if anyone's interested.

SATELLITE JACK'S REPORT

I. Old Walter

I interviewed Walter in his store. Utilizing the casual approach, I pretended to be there to ask his advice about music to use in creating DJ mixes.

A. Walter said that after our last visit, he pulled the copies of INSECT INVADERS off the racks.

   1. he indicated that he heard about the virus

   2. he said that he has never to his knowledge sold stolen or pirated merchandise and he never would

   3. he said that kids shouldn't waste their time on that game anyway

B. Walter claims he doesn't own a computer and has never been on the Internet.

   1. I tried to trip him up by asking if the Amazon thing was cutting into his business

   2. he gave me a strange look and said that to his knowledge there were no tall lady warriors in town

Comment: Walter appears to be in the clear because he does not have the means to create a computer virus. On the other hand, he's very crafty.

II. Stop the Insect Child Killers (S.I.C.K.)

Preliminary comment: One can only wonder what our society is coming to when people like this are allowed to set up a table and spread their antiquated views. Naturally, I believe in free speech. As you know, my parents started the Free Web Foundation to keep the Internet open and free. But shouldn't there be a word limit for losers like this? Like maybe 25 words or less?

Be that as it may, I spoke with the SICK leaders at their table in front of the Wham! retail establishment.

A. They believe that INSECT INVADERS, and computer games in general, are poisoning the minds of young people.

   1. the games are too violent

   2. they have no moral in the story line

   3. they distract kids from more constructive uses of time

B. Instead of playing computer games, kids should:

   1. read books

   2. play sports

   3. become robotic clones, so that adults can program them however they want to

   4. actually, I just made up that last one

C. SICK demands that Cye-Tek take INSECT INVADERS off the market and change the name of its game division (Terror Struck Games).

   1. as if!

   2. these people need to get a life

D. SICK wants to ban sales of the games to anyone under 21 years of age.

   1. I asked, Isn't this censorship?

   2. they said that maybe it's time for censorship: kids are not allowed to drive until a certain age, so why should they be allowed to shoot things?

   3. I didn't bother to point out the obvious flaw in their reasoning

E. One last bit of detective work: I "accidentally" left a wireless mike attached to their table. This allowed me to listen in on their conversation after I left. They seem to be planning some kind of protest against Cye-Tek tomorrow at the fair.

Final comment: This group is clearly hostile to the entertainment sector of the computer game industry. They have made INSECT INVADERS their special target. I believe that they would do anything to stop it. However, unless someone with some actual brains is helping them, their only weapons are screaming and shouting and petitions.

III. Kyle Purdue.

As many of you know, Kyle is a good friend of mine. I often trouble shoot for him in the computer lab. Needless to say, he was very busy at the First Annual High Tech Career Fair. But he took out a few minutes to talk to me.

A. He admitted that he programmed video games for Instinct Games in Texas.

    1. he coded an awesome game called GLOOM; it was revolutionary in its time

    2. suddenly, one day he realized that all he was using his brains for was death and destruction

    3. he decided to pay back his debt to society by becoming a computer teacher

    4. his philosophy is that new technology is a very poweful tool

        a. it can be used for good or evil

        b. he will fight to the end to use it for good

B. He recognizes the genius of INSECT INVADERS and can see why it is so popular.

    1. this is exactly what makes it so dangerous

    2. it's a prime example of the wonders of technology being misused for greed alone

C. He denied that he was a member of SICK.

D. Unfortunately, we were interrupted by some wart-for-brains who had no clue how to resolve an IRQ/device driver conflict. Kyle had to help him and our conversation came to an end.

Comment: I cannot help but agree with Kyle's assessment of INSECT INVADERS. It's a juvenile waste of time. Still, I can hardly believe that he would be involved in something so evil as creating the virus. Yet, there's no doubt he has a motive. He most certainly has the means. And I'm at a loss to explain that strange message, which he left at the warehouse. Sadly, I did not get a chance to ask him about it.

Appendix: (Below) A timeline of the events in this case, as we know them, to date.

Timeline

August 25: Annie's log = Acapulco
August 28: Annie's log = San Diego
August 30: first reported virus case in San Diego
September 2: Annie's log = Long Beach
September 3: first reported virus case in Los Angeles
September 4-18: shipping log matches up with reports of virus
September 8: Travis receives first payment
September 24: first e-mail from Skeet99
September 26: Annie at Dock 18
September 27: chased by blue pickup truck
September 28: investigate warehouse; encounter with Travis

September 29: school assembly for high tech career fair
September 30: interviews with suspects
October 1: last day of high tech fair
October 2: Exterminator virus fix to be released

You sit back and rub your eyes. It's late. But you still have work to do. You print out the timeline and type up your list of suspects. Then, you send an e-mail to the Digital Detectives—suggesting that you go to the high tech fair in the gym tomorrow. It opens at noon.

Cupping your chin in your hands, you stare blankly at the Suspect list. It feels like a thousand tiny particles of sand are grating between your eyes and eyelids. You wonder if you should just wait until tomorrow morning to work on the list and decide who still belongs under the Suspect heading, and who belongs under the Witness heading.

10

THE GLASS MASTER

After a good night's sleep, you rise late on Sunday morning. Your mind is much clearer now. You're ready to take on the high tech fair, the suspects, and whatever else is waiting out there.

The first thing you do is check your e-mail. Jack and Tina agree to meet at the park and then go to the fair. Randy says that he can't make it until later because he's got a soccer match, but good luck.

Just before noon, you set off to the park. Satellite Jack is already sitting at the table, pecking at his MicroJack. Tina rolls in at the same time you do.

"Have we all reviewed the reports?" Jack asks before you've even had time to lock your bike.

"Yes, Jack," you reply. "Yours was especially well organized. A+."

Jack frowns. "That's *not* why I asked. I just wanted to know where you think we are in the investigation."

"Well," you say, pulling the Suspect list out of your pack, "based on the reports, I was able to eliminate some of the suspects. Jason was a victim of the crime, so he's a witness. Walter didn't have the means to commit the crime, so we can move him to the Witness side, too. We all know about Travis. Here's the whole list."

You spread the paper on the table for the others to see.

SUSPECTS	WITNESSES
Mr. Purdue	Jason
Sandra Cye	Old Walter
Darren Cox	Travis
Bug Man (Arthur)	Russ Hodges
S.I.C.K.	other pirates
Annie (?)	

After Tina and Jack have studied the list, they each nod. They seem to agree with your choices. "So, who do you think did it?" Tina asks. "And why?"

"I'm glad the list is shorter, but I don't have any answers yet," you admit. "How about you?"

Tina pulls at the bill of her cap. "Me neither. We've got a lot of evidence, but it doesn't add up. At least, not to anything I can make out."

The two of you look at Jack. "I'm sure *you've* got a theory, Jack," you say.

He appears absorbed in his MicroJack. When he lifts his gaze, the look in his gray eyes somehow disarms you. "Yes, I have a theory," he says softly. "But that's all it is. I agree with you that we need to know more."

You wait, sure that Jack will expound his theory. But he doesn't. Very unusual, you think. He seems kind of down. Maybe he's miffed at not being keeper of the Suspect list. After your own struggles with it, you'd be just as happy to turn it over to him. Or, maybe he's just gotten a little more humble, and you should enjoy it while it lasts.

"So, what's our plan?" Tina demands.

"I guess just to keep our eyes and ears open," you say. "Ready to go to the gym?"

* * *

The high tech fair is basically a series of long folding tables arranged in a horseshoe shape in the gym. Sandra Cye, Darren Cox, and Russ Hodges have been given tables at the top of the shoe, along with Mr. Purdue's own table. About fifteen other organizations and companies have tables running along the sides, with computers, posters, and displays telling what they're all about.

Things are kind of quiet. "I guess it's still early," Tina says.

Kyle Purdue is off in a corner talking to Darren Cox. They both burst into laughter at something Darren says. But then, Kyle's mouth sets into a hard line when he sees the three of you.

"Jack," he calls, "may I speak to you?"

You and Tina try to blend into the wall as you edge close enough to listen in on the conversation.

Kyle's expression is unusually severe. "A computer in the lab is out of order. Do you happen to know what the problem is?"

"Somebody snitched on us," Tina whispers to you.

Jack stares at his brown shoes. He sets down his briefcase, shoves his hands into his pockets, and then looks Mr. Purdue right in the eye. "Yes."

"Explain, please."

"It fell victim to the INSECT INVADERS virus."

"And who's responsible for that? Who loaded the game on

to the computer?"

Jack draws himself up. "I did."

Kyle's arms fly up in rage. You've never seen him like this. "How could you *do* something like that? You know games are strictly forbidden! I'm *very* surprised at you, Jack."

"We...I mean, *I* was trying to crack the virus. Find out who made it."

"That's the stupidest thing I ever heard," Kyle fires back. "It's obvious Cye-Tek is at fault and they simply won't admit it."

Jack tilts his head. "Are you sure?

"This isn't your concern, Jack," Kyle responds. "I know you're smart, but something like this...you're in over your head."

"Yeah?" Jack challenges. "Well, maybe *you* can explain to *me*..."

But he doesn't have a chance to finish. A little kid runs up to Kyle. "Mr. Purduuuue," he whines, "Kerry won't let me play with the Mega Mantis!"

Kyle's face goes red. "Why do you want to play with that...*thing* anyway?"

The kid's face crumples like he's going to cry. Kyle realizes that he's made a mistake and reaches out an arm to comfort the kid. As he's leaving, he turns back to Jack. "We'll finish this later. That computer was school property. It's going to cost I-don't-know-what to replace..."

"Four thousand dollars," Jack says miserably.

His eyes follow Kyle as the teacher lets out a sudden sneeze and then walks away from him. Jack's face gradually turns from forlorn to resolute when you approach.

"You heard?" he says.

You and Tina nod glumly. You don't know what to say.

Jack stares off at the far wall. "Don't worry, guys. I'll take the fall. I'm the only one who'll be expelled."

Embarrassed, you gaze down at the floor. Wow, you think, you didn't know Jack had that kind of guts. You wonder if you'd do the same for him—or, if it comes down to it, if you may have to take him up on his offer.

Tina slaps his back. "Forget it. No one's getting expelled."

You feel a sudden glimmer of hope, too. "If we can catch the culprit, *they'll* have to pay for the computer."

"Right," Tina agrees. "Let's get to work."

* * *

You roam the tables at the fair, allowing your attention to drift. You're not sure exactly what you're looking for, but maybe, if you keep an open mind, it will just show up.

The Cye-Tek table isn't too crowded right now. Maybe the fans haven't arrived yet today. You wander over to it. Some younger kids are playing with the action figures: Mega Mantis, Killer Hopper, Black Locust, and Squish, the caterpillar. They've got Squish on the floor and the other insects are attacking him. "Splat! Splat! Splat!" the kids cry.

A young woman with brown hair is seated behind the table.

"Is Ms. Cye coming today?" you ask her.

"Yes, she'll be here in a few minutes. Can I help you?"

You decide to take a plunge. Maybe, she'll be more helpful to you than Sandra Cye was to Tina. "What's going on with that virus in the game?"

"It's been a pain," she admits. "But I think it's under control." She flips a glance at the Zeus table, next to Cye-Tek's. "These guys have developed a fix, if you need it."

"It's too late for us," you say.

Her face droops in sympathy. "Oh, I'm sorry. Were you using a bootleg? That's all right, you don't have to tell me. But honestly, I think it's the source of the virus. We've been spot checking our disks, and they don't have it."

She swats the air beside her head. There's an annoying sound, like a fly, that's been buzzing around the table since you got there. You thought that it might be part of their INSECT INVADERS promotion. Looking around, you don't see any flies.

At that moment, Sandra Cye comes bustling in. She's dressed with flawless good taste, and her expensive perfume precedes her.

Darren Cox watches her set down her bag and take off her suede jacket and cashmere scarf. He's dressed in a golf shirt and his usual shorts. "Good morning, Sandra," he greets her in a singsong voice.

She gives him a cold glance. "It's afternoon."

"Well, then it's about time you're out of bed."

"I was at a...never mind." She turns away from him.

"Emergency meeting?" Darren pipes up. "Cye-Tek's stock is in quite a tailspin, isn't it?"

Sandra ignores him. She flaps at the invisible buzzing fly. "Thanks, Anne," she says to the brown haired woman who gets up and pulls out a chair for her.

You glance over at Darren and the display that says:

Exterminator! Bug Killer!

"So are you guys working together to stamp out this virus?" you ask, knowing...hoping...you might stir up some trouble.

Darren grins. "Oh yes! Cye-Tek has been an *enormous* help to my company. Where would we be without you, Sandra?"

Sandra shakes her head with disgust. But then she grits her teeth and forces herself to smile at you. "We're very glad that Zeus is preventing kids' computers from being harmed, when they make the grave mistake of buying bootlegs."

By now Tina and Jack have joined you. Jack stands next to you, while Tina hangs back, eyeing Sandra Cye. "We just saw Travis," Jack whispers quietly in your ear. "From the look on his face, he's out for revenge."

You nod once, then turn your attention back to the debate in front of you.

"But we could be so much closer, Sandra," Darren says. He picks up a CD case and waves it in front of her. Inside is a clear disk. "I hold in my hand the glass master for Exterminator. Do I hear a bid?"

"The master copy," Jack murmurs in awe. "The one they use to stamp all the other CD-ROMs. It's made of glass."

"It can be yours for just a little bit of Cye-Tek stock," Darren continues. "Uh, did I say a little? I meant a lot, given the stock's current price."

Sandra glares at him. Russ Hodges leans in from the table on the other side of Darren and suggests, "It seems to me that it would make all the sense in the world for the two of you to team up."

Sandra folds her arms. "Thank you Mr. Hodges, but you don't know him like I do."

Darren turns to him with a smile. "She's a proud woman, Russ. The Queen Bee doesn't dance with just any old worker."

"The Queen is dead!" proclaims a voice behind you. "Long live the Queen!"

It's Arthur—Bug Man—shaking a finger in the air. He winks at you; you nod back.

Sandra shoots him a quick glare, then turns back to Darren. "You know, Darren, if sick people like the one who created this virus didn't exist, your company would be dead. How does that make you feel?"

"Welcome to the real world, Sandra," Darren replies. "I know you prefer fantasy. Reality gets your hands so dirty."

"The infestation is reality," Arthur warns darkly. He extends an arm and slowly opens his hand. Beetles swarm out of it.

Sandra jumps back in her chair, letting out a sharp gasp. "Oh! Get them away! I hate them!"

Darren laughs.

Kyle springs to his feet. "Arthur, what are you doing with those? This is unacceptable!"

Some kids squeal and scatter, while others whoop and chase after the beetles as they drop from Arthur's hand. Kyle gets up on his chair. It looks like he's about to leap over his table to tackle Arthur.

But something stops him. He's watching yet another commotion develop near the door. You follow his gaze.

A new influx of people is pouring into the gym. It's mostly adults, but they're also dragging a few kids with them. The adults are jabbing signs into the air, and soon you hear their chants.

"Stop the Insect Child Killers!"

"Cye-Tek go home!"

"Ban INSECT INVADERS!"

As the protesters press into the gym, you get squashed up against the edge of Kyle's table. Jack clings to your arm, and Tina holds on to his.

The throng is spearheaded by the earnest guy you talked to in the Wham! parking lot. He storms up to Sandra Cye's table. He's a lot less friendly to Sandra Cye than he was to you. His muscles look like their about to bust out of neck as he points a long finger at her.

"You ought to be ashamed of yourself!"

"Shame! Shame!" other protesters shout.

"The game is poison! A virus!" he shouts. "It's a contagion infecting our children!"

Sandra whirls in her seat, searching angrily for Kyle. He's retreated to the wall behind the tables. "Get them out of here!" she screams at him. He just lifts his palms in a helpless gesture.

A woman shakes her fist at Sandra. "You can't shut us up, lady. This is free speech!"

Meanwhile, Darren has clambered atop his table. He's motioning for the crowd to quiet down, with little success.

"Quiet!" Russ Hodges commands with unexpected authority. "You've made all the noise so far. Let someone else talk!"

Darren looks down, surprised. "Thanks, Russ." In the short lull that follows, he speaks to the protesters. "I understand your concerns. I used to make computer games myself. But with the games I made, I always tried to make sure there was a moral or educational angle to the story. Why don't you give Sandra a chance to defend the ethics of INSECT INVADERS?"

"Oh shut up, Darren," Sandra mutters.

"There is no defense!" the earnest man shouts.

"It's irresponsible to publish games like this!" someone else says.

"Hey!" Russ barks. "Now look, you proclaim your right to free speech. Why don't you give Ms. Cye *hers*?"

Sandra nods. "Thank you, Mr. Hodges, but honestly, I don't think I need to defend my game. Not to these people."

This brings on a whole new round of shouting. You look at Kyle. You can't believe he's doing nothing more than standing back, blowing his nose, and observing the spectacle.

Then a voice you know pierces the din. It's Travis, shouting, "No! You've got the wrong guy!"

Through the crowd, you spy Travis struggling with a protester. Kyle sees him, too. He dashes after Travis. What's going on? you wonder.

Travis spots Kyle and tries to fight his way through the protesters to the door. But hands keep grabbing at him, slowing him down. Travis desperately reaches out for a red handle—

BBBRRRRRIIIIIINGGGGG!!!

The fire alarm blares. People start to scream and rush for the exits. You're smushed even harder up against the table. You duck down and crawl under the table, bringing Jack and Tina with you.

108

Someone hits the lights on the way out, leaving you with only the murky daylight filtering in through the high gym windows. You clamp your hands to your ears, trying to shut out the deafening bell. Jack grimaces and cries, "Let's get out of here!"

But Tina has a big grin on her face. "NO!" she shouts. "Don't you see? This is our chance to do more investigating!"

You and Jack look at each other. "She's right," you say. "There's no fire. I saw Travis pull the alarm. He was just trying to escape Kyle. Let's wait here."

Two minutes later, after all the scuffling and chaos have ended, you're the only ones left in the gym. Thankfully, the fire alarm bell stops ringing.

Jack scrambles out from under the table. "They'll have to check the whole building for fire. It'll be a little while before they let people back in."

"Let's get busy!" Tina says.

DIGITAL
DETECTIVES

It's time for your final
investigation.

http://www.ddmysteries.com

and enter the key phrase **JOBFAIR**

When you've finished
this investigation, the
web site will give you
a page number
to return to.

11
THE ARREST

You scramble to put away your investigation tools. Once you've got them back in your pack, you grab Tina and Jack. "Let's hide under Hodges's table. He won't mind."

The three of you scoot along the floor to Russ's table. When enough of the crowd has filtered back in, you decide it's safe to stand up again. You turn, only to find yourself face to face with a man in a blue uniform!

The cop looks you up and down. No doubt about it, he's getting ready to ask some questions.

But then, Tina pops up next to you and he breaks into a smile. "Tina! What are you doing here?"

Tina returns a big, innocent smile and gestures around the gym. "Just learning about high tech!"

He nods. "Good. Good."

You can tell he's not sure what to say next, so you nudge Tina. "Oh!" she says. "Officer Gallegos, these are friends of mine." She introduces you and Jack, explaining to you, "My dad works with him sometimes."

"Are you here because of the fire alarm?" you ask, shaking the officer's hand.

"Yep," he confirms. "Someone phoned in about the protesters, too."

"They claimed they were just exercising their right to free

speech," Jack says.

"Well, they can't be disrupting a school sponsored function," Officer Gallegos says.

"So, nobody's getting arrested?" Tina ventures.

"Just the person who pulled the fire alarm. Any of you see anything?"

You shift uncomfortably. Luckily, Tina is thinking fast. "I think there might be another crime," she says. "A bigger one."

The officer's eyebrows lift. Instinctively, his hand touches the gun at his side. "What's that?"

"You know that computer game, INSECT INVADERS?" Tina replies. "Well, there are some pirates selling illegal copies of it."

Officer Gallegos nods.

"But the crime is really much worse," Jack breaks in. "The bootleg copies contain a virus that destroys the hard drives on kids' computers."

"That's bad," the policeman agrees.

"We've been gathering evidence on it," Tina adds. "I think we have enough by now to name the perp."

You squeeze Tina's arm to slow her down. "But we need to review the evidence first, before we know for sure. Right, guys?"

Tina and Jack nod. Officer Gallegos grants an indulgent smile. "All righty, then. I'll be right here. My partner, Officer Pardelli, is on the other side of the gym. You just let us know."

You find a corner in the back of the gym, where you can sit down with your fellow agents. Jack pulls his laptop out of his briefcase. You bring the crime lab up on the screen.

"There you are!" a voice calls out. It's Randy, in his sweat-suit. "I've been looking all over for you."

"You're here just in time," you say. "We're just about to figure out who did the crime."

Randy sits down to join you, and you begin your review.

It's time to name the culprit.
Go to:

http://www.ddmysteries.com
and enter the key phrase **LAB**

Do not read ahead!

"Okay," you announce. "I think I know who it is."

You've discussed your choice with the other three Digital Detectives. Not everyone agrees with you. They each have their favorite theory, and you've been taking all their ideas into account. But since you've got the Suspect list, you're the one who has to make the final decision.

Tina stands up. She tugs her cap firmly down on her head and says, "Let's go."

You march up to Officer Gallegos. "We've figured out who it is," Tina tells him.

Gallegos regards her carefully, then turns his gaze to the rest of you. "You look like you're serious about this. All right, you tell me who it is, and we'll look into it."

"Kyle Purdue," you declare.

Gallegos nods and signals to his partner across the room. You and the other Digital Detectives follow him over to Kyle's table where Pardelli joins you. The two officers flank Kyle. "Mr. Purdue," Officer Gallego declares. "We have a problem. These young people tell us that you may be the person who has been spreading a computer virus."

Kyle looks stunned. "What?" he cries. He regards you with a hurt expression, as Gallego waits for you to explain.

Suddenly, the whole gym has fallen silent. All eyes

are on you. You take a deep breath.

"The first thing we asked ourselves was," you say, "what was the motive for the crime? Mr. Purdue has let it been known that he disapproves of Cye-Tek, and especially, INSECT INVADERS. We have evidence that he's in league with the Stop the Insect Child Killers group."

"All right!" some SICK person calls out. Kyle glares at them.

"So, there's his motive for sabotaging the game," you go on. "Second, we asked if Mr. Purdue had the means to commit the crime. We've learned that he was once a programmer for a game company in Texas."

"Not just any company," Jack puts in. "But the legendary Instinct Games."

Kyle stares at Jack with a terribly confused and injured look. "Jack, you couldn't possibly believe I'd do something like this. It's the opposite of everything I stand for!"

"Finally," you say, "we have evidence that connects him to the distribution of the pirate game. He left a message at the warehouse, where the bootlegs are stored. There was a computer disk there with his fingerprints on it. Also, he's been sneezing all day, and we found cold pills at the warehouse"

"I don't have a cold!" Kyle bursts out. "It's allergies."

He pulls a vial of allergy medication from his pock-et and waves it in your face. "I have nothing to do with this virus, other than trying to stop it and the bootleg game that's spreading it!"

"It's true."

You look up. Travis steps out from behind a knot of people. "I know you don't like me, Mr. Purdue, but I can't let you take the rap for this."

You gape in surprise. A sinking feeling comes over you as Travis explains. "That disk you found at the warehouse is one that I, er, borrowed from Mr. Purdue's desk. I thought it might have information about SICK. All Mr. Purdue was doing was trying to stop the bootleg games. That's why he called the warehouse, and that's why we had information on him there. That's also why he chased after me, just a few minutes ago. He figured that it was bad enough Cye-Tek was making all that money off of kids, but worse if more copies of the game were being sold cheaply."

Sandra Cye jumps to her feet with indignation. "Young man, do you mean to say..."

"Gotta go!" Travis calls, and dashes from the room.

This has to be the most embarrassing moment in your life. Your ears burn, knowing the entire crowd in the gym is witness to your mistake. You turn to Kyle. "I don't know what to say, Mr. Purdue. I'm really,

really sorry..."

You hope that maybe when you can explain everything, he'll forgive you. But for now, he responds only with a hard, disappointed stare.

Oops! Try naming the culprit again. Go to:

http://www.ddmysteries.com

and enter the key phrase **LAB**

117

"Okay," you announce. "I think I know who it is."

You've discussed your choice with the other three Digital Detectives. Not everyone agrees with you. They each have their favorite theory, and you've been taking all their ideas into account. But since you've got the Suspect list, you're the one who has to make the final decision.

Tina stands up and says, "Let's go."

You march up to Officer Gallegos. "We've figured out who it is," Tina tells him.

Gallegos regards her carefully, then turns his gaze to the rest of you. "You look like you're serious about this. All right, you tell me who it is, and we'll look into it."

"It's Sandra Cye," you tell him.

"Figures!" Tina snorts.

Gallegos raises his eyebrows way up on his forehead. But instead of questioning you, he signals to his partner across the room. You and the other Digital Detectives go with him to Sandra's table. Pardelli arrives, and the two officers flank her.

"Ms. Cye, these young people think they've fingered the culprit responsible for the virus that is causing so much trouble for your game," Gallegos says in a firm voice.

This catches the attention of the people around you. Soon the entire gym falls silent. Everyone is waiting for you to say who it is.

"It's Sandra Cye herself!" you declare.

Sandra's eyes go wide with disbelief. "Are you insane?" she sputters.

"You had the means," you reply. "You can't deny that you had the opportunity, too."

Sandra gets all red in face. "Of course, I had the means and the opportunity. It's my company, you doofus! What possible motive could I have for committing this crime? Do you realize how much my net worth has fallen in the past week?!"

"Hmm, she's got a point," Randy murmurs to you.

"Yeah, and we didn't find her fingerprints at the dock or in the warehouse," Jack points out.

Your face drops. Great. *Now* he tells you.

Tina finishes off your embarrassment by adding, "I think we might need to go back to the drawing board."

"Uh, okay." You turn to Sandra. "Maybe I made a mistake," you say lamely. "Sorry. Let me consult with my friends again."

Sandra folds her arms and stomps her foot. "Get it right this time, will you?"

Oops! Try naming the culprit again. Go to:

http://www.ddmysteries.com

and enter the key phrase **LAB**

"I think I know who did it," you announce.

"Who is it?" Randy asks.

You tell them your choice, and Tina immediately makes a face. "No. No way. It couldn't be."

"Hey!" you object. "I'm the keeper of the Suspect list. I thought it was up to me to make the decision."

"True," Jack agrees, "but I'm afraid I have to agree with Tina. You're off on this one. I think you should reconsider."

You look at Randy. "Sorry," he says gently. "But I think they're right. We don't want to go accusing the wrong person."

You let out a sigh. "All right," you agree, "I'll go back and take a look at the evidence again."

Go back to the crime lab and try again!

http://www.ddmysteries.com
and enter the key phrase **LAB**

"Okay," you announce. "I think I know who it is."

You've discussed your choice with the other three Digital Detectives. Not everyone agrees with you. They each have their favorite theory, and you've been taking all their ideas into account. But since you've got the Suspect list, you're the one who has to make the final decision.

Tina stands up. She tugs her cap firmly down on her head and says, "Let's go."

You march up to Officer Gallegos. "We've figured out who it is," Tina tells him.

Gallegos regards her carefully, then turns his gaze to the rest of you. "You look like you're serious about this. All right, you tell me who it is, and we'll look into it."

"Darren Cox," you say.

Gallegos nods and signals to his partner across the room. You and the other Digital Detectives follow him over to Darren's table. Pardelli arrives, and the two officers come up on either side of him. "Darren Cox?"

"Yeah, so?" Darren responds.

"These young people claim to have evidence that you are the person who has been spreading a computer virus via illegal pirated copies of the game INSECT INVADERS," Gallegos says.

"What? That's outrageous!"

Cox's exclamation is so loud that the whole gym falls silent. All eyes turn to you. You take a deep breath. Darren regards you with a smirk of disdain as you begin.

You start by explaining the nature of the crime to the few people in the gym who haven't heard about it yet. When that's done, you lay out your case.

"The first thing we asked was, what could be the motive for this crime? A possible motive is that it was done by someone who doesn't like kids and computers very much. That's not true of Darren, but we think he had a much stronger motive. Our evidence shows that he's had a feud going with Sandra Cye for a long time. His motive was to sabotage the game, ruin Sandra's company, and make a lot of money besides."

Darren rolls his eyes and blows air through his lips.

Randy helps you out. "The evidence was in a folder on Sandra Cye's table. Sorry for snooping, Ms. Cye, but I think you'll be glad we did. It looks like you and Darren have known each other for a long time, right? Darren was very big in the computer game business once, but he was outdone by newer companies like yours."

Sandra looks at Darren with a mock frown. "Sad, but true."

"You'd be nowhere without me," Darren retorts. "But none of this proves that I created this virus."

"You had the means to," you say. "Not only were you once a game programmer, you know all about computer viruses. No one is more qualified than you to plant a virus like this."

Darren shrugs it off. "So I'm smart! Big deal!"

"Yes. Neither the motive nor the means prove you did it," you allow. "But you also had the opportunity. Our evidence shows that not only did you take it, but you're the only one who could have masterminded the crime."

Darren taps his foot impatiently. "This is ridiculous," he says to Officer Gallegos. "You're not going to make me stand here and listen to this noise from a bunch of kids, are you?"

Gallegos smiles slowly. "Sure I am."

"We have three types of evidence to connect Darren to the

crime," you continue. "First, we have fingerprints and foot-prints. They link you to the dock where the pirated disks came in, and to the warehouse where they were stored. Second, we have written evidence: your account books, shipping logs, and so on."

Jack steps forward. "But it's the third clue that cinches it. We found it on the glass master copy of Exterminator."

He holds up the case containing the master. You notice Sandra sneaking a peek into her briefcase.

"Which we, um, found in Ms. Cye's briefcase," you confess. "We checked the history of this program, Mr. Cox. You start-ed working on it, on August 12, ten days before the first virus hit. How could you have been working on the cure before anyone even knew there was a disease? Anyone but *you*, that is, because you designed the virus!"

Darren is barely listening to you any more. Instead, his fury is fixed on Sandra. "Thief!" he accuses.

She jumps to her feet. You can practically see the steam coming out of her ears. "Oh, listen to you! You nearly destroyed my company! You pathetic—"

She lunges for Darren. As Officer Pardelli restrains her, Darren steps forward and unleashes a tirade at Sandra. "You are such an ingrate! I gave you your start, but did that mean anything? No! Instead, you stab me in the back, then throw me a few little crumbs — two measly scenes for the game. I guess I showed you that I've still got some chops, didn't I?"

Gallegos gets the handcuffs out. He pins Darren's arms and slaps on the cuffs. "That's enough of that." He and Pardelli hustle Darren out of the room.

Sandra Cye's face flushes crimson as she realizes how much

she's revealed about herself to the world. She slumps slowly into her chair, shaking.

But when you look out at the gawking crowd, you realize that it's not her they're staring at. It's you, and Tina and Randy and Jack. It dawns on you that their expressions are gapes of amazement—that the four of you have solved the mystery of the killer insect virus.

One by one, you turn to each other. Smiles begin to crawl across your faces. Suddenly, Kyle Purdue is there, pumping your hand in congratulations. Russ Hodges is doing the same. Before you know it, the whole gym is clapping.

Tina stands back to take it all in for a minute. Then she leaps into the air and shouts, "We did it!"

12
LOOSE ENDS

Tina's father lifts a slender glass into the air. Golden bubbles of sparkling apple cider twinkle in the dining room light.

"To the Digital Detectives!" he declares.

You, Randy, Tina, and Jack clink your glasses, your eyes aglow with the success of your first case. Then, you dive into the meal in front of you.

Mr. Garrett promised to cater a gourmet meal for you—anything you wanted. To his dismay, you unanimously agreed on pizza. The gourmet part would be that it had everything on it.

"I spent the afternoon with a police detective," Tina's dad—he likes you to call him by his first name, Frank—says. "They've pretty much got the case wrapped up. Do you want to hear the details?"

Amid your chorus of Yeses, Jack's voice can be heard saying, "Nah, I've already got 'em all figured out."

He's immediately pelted with olives. Even Tina's dad joins in.

"Let's hear the details," Randy repeats eagerly. "I'll post them on our web site. We're already getting twenty times as many hits as usual, since I first posted the Digital Detectives story."

"All right," Frank says, "here's what the detective told me.

By the time they got him down to the station, Darren had clammed up. So, they got a search warrant for the Zeus office and computer files. Turned up plenty of evidence proving Darren's the one. The other employees weren't in on it, but they confirmed that they'd started work on the virus cure before anyone knew there was a virus."

"So, were we right about his motive?" you say. "He had something against Cye-Tek?"

"Something big," Frank confirms. "Darren and Sandra were once a couple. It's true that he gave her her start in the game business. It's also true that she turned on him. She pretty much crushed his game company out of existence. Darren must have been thinking about his revenge for a long time. When Sandra farmed out a couple of little scenes for INSECT INVADERS to him—and I think she did that just to make him feel even smaller—he saw his chance."

"Plus, he wanted to make a pile of money," Tina points out.

"True," her father agrees. "Zeus wasn't doing so well before Exterminator."

"What about Skeet?" Randy wonders.

"They got him. Sad story. He's an old fisherman who used to fish with my father, as a matter of fact." Tina's family has been in Crescent Bay for four generations. They were all fishermen until recently, when the bay became overfished. "He couldn't make a living from the sea anymore, so I guess he turned to this. He'll get a reduced sentence, though, for testifying against Darren."

"Do you know why he went away for those two days?"

"Well, it's lucky for you kids that he did. Otherwise, who knows what would have happened to you at that warehouse?

He went up to San Francisco to get some advance copies of Exterminator, so that Darren could sell them at the fair."

"Is Travis going to jail, too?" you ask.

"I think he'll get probation," Frank answers. "He's going to be a witness for the prosecution as well."

Suddenly, Jack is spitting pizza out of his mouth.

"What's the matter?" Tina demands. "Do you think Travis should be in prison?"

"No," he says, curling his tongue over and over. "There are green peppers on this pizza."

"I warned you!" Tina says. "We got them on half of one of the pies."

Jack looks through the pizza boxes. It's the only half left, so Jack picks the green peppers off the remainder of his piece and continues eating.

"I've also got some good news for you all," Frank continues when things have calmed down. "Darren's company will pay to replace the school computer that was destroyed by the virus."

This brings a cheer from all four of you. You raise your glasses for another toast. "What a relief," you say, clinking.

"Is Kyle still mad at you, Jack?" Randy asks.

"I think he's getting over it," Jack replies breezily.

"Jack!" Tina sits upright, as if about to scold him. Her face melts into a smile. "I'm glad to see your supreme confidence has returned."

"Yeah, I went offline for a little while there," he admits.

Tina frowns again. "There's one more thing we never found out. It's been bugging me and bugging me. Who the heck is Annie?"

"Didn't you see the photo in Sandra's folder?" Jack answers. "It's not a *who*, it's a *what*."

"Right, Jack," Frank says. "The *Sweet Annie* was Darren's yacht. Not really even his, because he still owed so much money on it. It was the vessel used to distribute the pirate copies of the game up and down the coast. I'd be willing to bet that as soon as Exterminator made enough money to pay off the boat, he'd sail her off to some tropical place and let the profits pile up."

"So who gets Exterminator now?" you wonder.

"Cye-Tek has already made an offer for what's left of Zeus Protection Systems," Frank replies.

Tina groans. "That just doesn't seem fair. Okay, Darren Cox committed a crime, but should Sandra Cye be the one who gets the benefit?"

Her father shakes his head in agreement. "It's a cut-throat business, honey.

Suddenly, Jack starts jumping up and down in his chair and talking with his mouth full of pizza. "Hey, I almoft forgot to tell 'ou." He swallows. "We benefit, too. I found out from Kyle, just when I was leaving school, that Cye-Tek is going to give us a reward!"

Another round of cheers rises from the table. Everyone starts babbling at once about what to do with the money.

Jack puts out his arms. "Hold it, hold it," he commands, "I know what to do with it. You all haven't forgotten already that we started a detective agency, have you? We need to invest the money into new technology."

"Wait a minute! I want to get a new wetsuit with that money," you object.

"I'm sure *some* of the reward money will be divided among each of you individually," Frank suggests. "Won't it, Jack?"

Jack nods reluctantly. Then he starts bouncing up and down with excitement again, as he describes the new tools he can devise. "I can modify the scanner so it does handwriting analysis. And make a digital dropper that will give us blood analysis right on the spot."

"Cool," Randy says. "All we need is a new case."

"There'll be more," Tina says. She holds each of you around the table in turn with her gaze. "The Digital Detectives are just beginning."

You think about all the strange things you uncovered in the course of your investigation. You think about what Tina's dad called the cut-throat nature of the high tech world. You think about what else might be waiting for you out there.

"Yep," you agree, "there's sure to be another case."

ABOUT THE AUTHOR

Jay Montavon lives in San Francisco. He has written more than twenty books and computer games under different pen names, including a number of books in the *Choose Your Own Adventure* series, and the computer games: *Journey into the Brain* and *3D Castle Creator*. He's hard at work on a new *Digital Detectives Mystery*.

When Nightmares Come True

Digital Detectives™ Mystery #2

A missing surfer.
An abandoned mansion.
A deadly secret...

When a surfer disappears near one of the creepiest beach-front mansions in Crescent Bay, the Digital Detectives stumble onto their next big mystery. The house once belonged to an eccentric scientist, Tibias Mandrake, who performed some very bizarre experiments in his laboratory. But now that the house is on the real estate market, some people in Crescent Bay are *dying* to get their hands on it....

To solve the mystery, you'll make on-line investigations of the mansion, a pitch-black cave, and Mandrake's secret lab. Analyze every fingerprint, interrogate every suspect, and record everything in your on-line crime journal. Remember: if you miss a single clue, you might not live to solve another case.

Available now in bookstores!